LOVE DELIVERED

BOOK 4 IN THE FAITH IN LOVE SERIES

GINA JOHNSON

DEDICATION

*To Karl. My biggest cheerleader and my number one fan.
Your love for me is intoxicating and I'm a ready recipient.
Thanks for sacrificing so much for me, honey. I'm honored to
be your Mrs. I love you!*

ACKNOWLEDGMENTS

To my Lord and Savior Jesus Christ. Thank you for always pursuing me. Thank you for teaching me through your Word, and thank you for those awesome little blessings that you give me to let me know that I'm never forgotten. Father, I owe you my life. Use me as your vessel for your glory!

To Cierra, Tre', Joshua, and Micah. You four are my hearts. My greatest of accomplishments, my grandest of joys. Nothing makes me happier than knowing that you four are filled with joy always. I hope you each smile each day for the rest of your lives. Mommy loves you with everything that is within me, and all of this is for you. I love you my beautiful and smart babies! Always keep God first!

To Michelle Stimpson. Thank you for being such an

amazing sister-in-Christ, friend, and mentor. You rolled out the red carpet for me in Dallas and I'll never forget it! Thanks for entrusting me to take Faith and Blaise to new places all by myself! Many don't realize this, but I'm honored to have a front-row seat. You are a legend! I love you!

To Keleigh Crigler Hadley. There aren't enough adequate words to describe what you mean to me, especially with this project. This very delicate and special project.Thank you for encouraging me, for talking me off the ledge, for helping me identify the holes in my plots, for talking to me on the phone late at night and early in the morning. Thank you for praying with me, laughing with me and for being the best literary midwife in the entire world! I couldn't have done this without you sis! I love you to life! Salute!

To Tabitha Matthews. Thanks for being my sounding board when life gets crazier than it is on an ordinary day. Thanks for making me laugh, for praying with me and for speaking life into me. I love you sis.

To Angie Green. My BFF of 39 years! Girl you already know! You are the bearer of my secrets, the person who defends me no matter what! Thank you for being so proud of me and for cheering me on along the way. I love you sis! Forever and Always!

To Mom and Dad. Thanks for your love, and consistency. Thanks for giving me the best childhood ever. Thanks for showing me what it means to love God and to truly succeed at what matters most. I hope I'm making you proud of me. I'm trying and I love you both more than all of the stars in all of the galaxies.

To Uncle Stan. My favorite Unc who just so happens to be my coolest Unc. Thanks for all of your support and counsel. It means the world to me. I love you!

To Gee, Gemel, Chantel and Brittany. Thanks for loving me and supporting me. I love you all more than you know!

To Mom and George. Thanks for coming through for me in the clutch. Thanks for always being understanding and letting me be myself. Thanks for raising my husband to be so amazing. You're the best in-laws ever! I love you!

To Sisters in Christ book club. Thank you for your warm hospitality and love offering. I can't wait to come back! I hope you enjoy this book and get a kick out of a few of the new characters!

To Chanda and Vanessa. Ya'll being so proud of me, means the world to me. Thank you to my forever big sisters. I love you both dearly, even when we fuss and argue!

To my CML's Proverbs 27:17. Thanks for sharpening me sisters. I love each of you!

To my Connection Church Family. Thanks for welcoming me in with open arms. I love each of you.

To my Pastor Lamarr Lark and First Lady(smile) Brenda, thank you for all of your encouragement and support!

To Latavia and Jon! So glad that God brought us into each other's lives! Love you both!

To Jeida Walker and Kp Holley. I love you sister scribes! Thanks for kicking it with me while I was in Dallas! Let's do it again!

To Paw Paw. Thanks for being the best grandfather on earth! I love you so much!

CHAPTER 1

The joy beating in sync with my heart after giving Blaise the news that we had finally conceived was suddenly replaced with fear and confusion. Blaise walked back into the living room like he had seen a ghost.

"Who was at the door? Are the movers here? What's wrong Blaise?" I asked.

Blaise took a deep breath and spoke each word one at a time like he was reciting a poem for a school play.

"Faith, baby. The person at the door is still there. They--"

"Well, who is it?" I asked, cutting Blaise off.

"It's a woman. She says she's your mother."

I was confused beyond words. "What do you mean my mother? You mean my biological mother?"

Blaise shrugged. "I'm assuming that's what she meant."

I took off toward the front door, being careful not to trip over any of the boxes in my empty living room and Blaise followed close behind. "Are you alright babe?"

"I'm fine," I replied. "Clearly someone is trying to play a joke, but it's not funny. My biological mother is dead."

When I got to the front door and saw the woman standing there, I gasped. Looking at her was like looking into a mirror from the future. Aside from the silver hair and crow's feet, she looked exactly like me. If she wasn't my biological mother, she was definitely a relative.

"May I help you?" I asked.

Tears welled up in the woman's eyes. "My God, you're more beautiful than I imagined you'd be."

"I'm sorry, but I didn't get your name," I said, in a matter of fact tone.

"Where are my manners?" she said. "Forgive me. My name is Sheila Green."

"How can I help you, Sheila?" I asked.

"I don't know how to say this, but…well…" She took a deep breath and continued. "I'm the woman who gave birth to you."

At that moment I remembered where I'd first heard Sheila's name. It was at Granny C's nursing home with Daddy. We were both visiting her and my heart was broken because her Alzheimer's had stolen her memories of who I was. Instead of recognizing me as her granddaughter she had called me Sheila and that's when my father had confessed to me that his wife, who I grew up thinking was my mother, was actually not my mother at all. He told me that my birth mother was a woman named Sheila and that he had had an affair with her. She kept her pregnancy a secret from him, but he later found out about me when Sheila's mother reached out to my dad saying that Sheila had died shortly after giving birth. My dad was shocked and agreed to raise me because Sheila's mother said she wasn't capable of raising a newborn and if he didn't raise me, I'd end up being a ward of the state.

All of those memories were swirling around in my head as I locked eyes with this woman who said she was my mother. The woman my father told me was dead. Yet here she stood. I wanted to believe that she was lying because if she wasn't that would mean that my father had deceived me. Again.

CHAPTER 2

FAITH

*I*t was true. I knew it. And I didn't need genetic testing or any other kind of testing to prove it. As much as I didn't want to believe what the woman at my door was saying, I was the spitting image of her and knew that she was indeed my biological mother.

The reality of the situation caused the room to spin and my knees to weaken.

Blaise rushed to my side as I burst into tears. "Faith, baby you alright?"

"No," I cried.

"What do you need?" Blaise asked with pain in his eyes.

"I just need some water."

Blaise wrapped his arms around me and led me away from the door where Sheila was still standing and to a chair sitting near all of the boxes in the living room. He looked at me again and said, "Will you be ok right here while I go get you some water?"

I nodded.

Blaise went to the kitchen to get a bottle of water and the living room door was still open while Sheila stood there standing like a statue.

Blaise handed me the water and knelt down in front of me. He leaned in and spoke just above a whisper.

"You call it, baby. If you want me to ask her to leave, I will. If you want me to invite her inside, I will. It's up to you."

I took a sip of water and tried willing myself to speak, but words wouldn't form. Only tears. Blaise held me as my entire body shook from weeping.

"It's going to be ok," Blaise whispered. "I promise it's going to be ok."

I finally gathered myself enough to speak. "I guess invite her in," I sniffed.

Blaise never let go of me, and called out toward the living room door, "Sheila! Come on in, ma'am."

Sheila walked in slowly and covered her mouth when she saw me trembling with tears still raining down my face.

"As you can imagine, this is extremely shocking for her," Blaise said.

Sheila nodded her head in agreement. "I'm so sorry."

I looked up at Sheila again as fresh tears streamed down my cheeks. I didn't know what to say. I didn't know what to think. There was an awkward silence and that made me even more anxious.

Blaise broke the silence by saying, "So Sheila. Um, how did you find Faith?"

"I found her online. All I knew was her name and after searching through several different online data-bases, I was able to narrow down the search. You'd be surprised by how many Faith Caldwells there are in Texas." A nervous giggle escaped her lips.

Sheila's timing was impeccable. After owning my home for five years, I was moving to Atlanta with Blaise and had she come to my home just one day later, I would have already been gone. I still made a mental note to take extra precautions to assure that my personal information from here on out was kept private.

"So…" Sheila said. "It looks like you're moving?"

"We sure are," Blaise replied. "After being married for about eight months, I was finally able to convince her to sell this house and move in with me." Blaise chuckled alone.

I took a deep breath and finally willed myself to speak. "Sheila, you'll have to pardon me. I'm just abso-lutely in shock. I was told that you were dead."

"I know," Sheila said, hanging her head. "That was what my mother told your father."

"Why would she lie to him?" I sniffed.

"Because…" Sheila hesitated. "I was out of it, and I knew I wouldn't be able to care for a baby." Another pause. "So I asked my mother to care for you, but my mother was old and sickly and she didn't think that she could care for you either, so she contacted your father and told him that I was dead. She was afraid that if he knew I was alive, he would refuse to care for you because of….well...because…"

"Because he already had a family of his own?" I added while swiping more tears from my face.

"Well yes," Sheila replied. "And I'm not proud of that."

"So," I stammered. "What made you come looking for me now? After all these years?"

Sheila took a deep breath like she was working up the nerve to speak her next words.

"I've lived a rough life over the years and while I've been wanting to find you for a long time, I knew I couldn't do it until I got myself together."

"I have to be honest with you Sheila," I said. "This is a lot of information to process and I need some time to wrap my mind around all of this."

"I understand," Sheila said, nodding her head in agreement. "In the meantime," she hesitated. "Can we at least exchange phone numbers? That way we can keep in touch?"

I looked up at Blaise, and he mouthed the words, *It's your call.*

I turned to face Sheila and said, "That will be fine. But first...can we take your picture? Just to confirm who you are with my father?"

"That's understandable," Sheila said.

Blaise stood up, took Sheila's picture, and walked her to the door.

"Thank you so much for your kindness," Sheila said, walking out of the door.

"No problem," Blaise replied.

The strength had not yet returned to my legs, so all I could do was sit in the chair in the living room, still in shock.

My biological mother, also known as my father's ex-mistress had returned from the dead.

CHAPTER 3

By the time Blaise returned from seeing Sheila to the door, I was on the phone with Daddy.

"How's my baby girl?" Daddy asked in a chipper tone.

My voice trembled as I replied, "Upset."

"Upset about what?"

"My biological mother just came to my house."

"What are you talking about Faith?"

"As Blaise and I were waiting for the movers to arrive, there was a knock on the door. Blaise opened the door and the woman standing there told him that her name was Sheila and that she is my birth mother."

"Someone is playing a prank," Daddy said. "Sheila died when you were a few days old. Her mother told me it was a blood clot that killed her."

"I thought you might say that," I said. "Blaise, can you text Daddy the picture of Sheila that you just took?"

A beat later the picture appears on Daddy's phone. "Well I'll be," Daddy said. "That *is* Sheila. I don't believe this."

I could hear Mom in the background say, "What's going on Jed?"

"It turns out that Faith's birth mother is still alive," Daddy said. "She just went by Faith's house."

Mama was silent after that, and I could only imagine the thoughts running through her mind. She had just recently gotten to the place where she fully forgave Daddy, so I hoped this turn of events wouldn't cause a setback in their healed marriage.

"I don't know what to say." Daddy mumbled.

"What should I do, Daddy? Sheila said she'd like us to get to know each other."

Daddy's tone was skeptical. "What made her come back around now after all these years is my question."

"I'm not sure, but I don't think I can just ignore her now."

"Be careful Faith," Daddy warned.

"I will Daddy," I said, drying my face with more kleenex. "I just don't feel right completely turning my back on her."

"I trust you baby girl, but please proceed with caution."

When I hung up with Daddy, Blaise was outside directing the movers. He came in and I was still sitting in the middle of the living room floor in a daze.

He wiped sweat from his brow and said, "What can I do for you baby? Anything. You don't need to be stressed right now. That may upset the baby," he leaned over and rubbed my stomach.

The baby. With the whirlwind of emotions, I had just experienced, I had forgotten briefly, that I was carrying a baby in my womb.

Tears stung my eyes.

"What's wrong?" Blaise asked with concern.

"I was just thinking about the happiest day of my life--our wedding. And how at the end of the reception I had to be rushed to the hospital with complications from endometriosis, and then on the second happiest day of my life--after finding out that I'm finally pregnant, my biological mother shows up out of nowhere, creating all kinds of confusion and doubt. Why can't I ever just enjoy life without drama?"

Blaise held both of my hands and said, "Let's pray."

I bowed my head as my husband went to the throne on my behalf.

"Father, this day has definitely taken a turn. We went from rejoicing and elated to confused and fearful. But Father we know that you are not the author of confusion and we also know that you did not give us the spirit of fear. So with that in mind please help us to remember that nothing takes you by surprise and that we are in the palm of your hand, no matter what. Please comfort Faith's heart right now, and enable her to enjoy every blessing that is due her. In Jesus' name, I pray, Amen."

CHAPTER 4

"*F*aith shut up!"

     I held the phone away from my ear as Kya expressed her surprise over Sheila's resurrection.

"I know girl," I said with a sigh.

"And when did all of this happen?" Kya asked.

"A couple of weeks ago."

"And you're just now telling me?"

"It was so overwhelming I couldn't bring myself to share it with anyone for a while."

"Girl. Are you all alright? This is a lot to go through all at once. Moving away from your hometown, selling your house, finding out that you're pregnant, and starting your new job in your new city with the knowledge that your biological mom who you thought was dead is really alive? Girl this needs to go in a book!"

"I know," I said, munching on a saltine cracker. "My life is filled with drama."

"But your life is filled with blessings too," Kya said. "You're married to the man of your dreams, you live in a beautiful home, you have a great job as a loan officer at one of the largest banks in Atlanta, and your dream of making Blaise a father is coming true. For someone whose life is filled with drama, God sure has made up for it, in the blessing department."

"Listen to you, sounding all spiritual," I chuckled.

"I've been dating this guy who insists that I go to church with him and I think it's rubbing off on me."

"Well good for you! And you didn't tell me that you were dating! Spill the tea!"

I leaned back in the plush chair in my office, slipped off my heels and propped my feet up on my desk. Swiveling my chair a few inches to the left, I took in the view of downtown Atlanta from the picture window that was the backdrop of the best office I had ever had.

I could hear the joy in Kya's voice as she described her new boo.

"Faith he's like no other man I've ever met."

"Where'd you meet him?"

"Girl, standing in a long line at the grocery store. I was reading a magazine to pass the time, and when I tried to put the magazine back I knocked the whole display over. I was so embarrassed."

"Oh no," I said, grinning. "And then, let me guess. He helped you pick all the magazines up?"

"He sure did. And as we were both on the floor in

the checkout line picking up magazines he struck up a conversation and made me laugh. I told him thanks for the laugh because I needed it. He asked me why and I told him I had had a stressful day at work. Then get this. He asked me if he could pray for me."

I almost fell out of my swivel chair. "Girl get out!"

"I know Faith! I almost died. When I told him yes, he prayed for me right there in the grocery store and then told me he'd like to keep in touch so that I could keep him posted on God answering his prayer."

"What?" I shrieked.

"Girl yes. I gave him my social media handles and he DM'd me the next day asking me if God had answered his prayer. The tripped out part? He did. The next day at work a new girl was hired and that helped lessen my load tremendously. When I told him God answered his prayer, he invited me to church and I went and really enjoyed it. I started going each week after that."

I squealed as Kya continued.

"After two weeks of communicating with him through DM's, and going to his church two Sundays in a row, he invited me to lunch after service. We talked like we had known each other forever."

I grabbed a Kleenex. "Girl, you're about to make me cry."

Kya hollered. "Faith, you're pregnant. Everything makes you cry."

I giggled. "What does he do for a living and what does he look like?"

"You'll never believe it," Kya exclaimed.

"What?"

"He's a youth pastor and he's under six feet tall."

"A youth pastor? And you threw out your height requirement?"

"For him, I did."

"Then he must be built like Idris Elba," I said.

"Not exactly," Kya replied. "He's built more like Ice Cube."

"Who are you and what have you done with my friend Kya?"

"Shut up," Kya snickered. "I'm just learning that a lot of that stuff that really mattered to me, doesn't matter at all. This guy doesn't make six figures and he's not ripped like a model, but he loves God. He prays with me, he's polite, and he treats me like I'm his sunshine on a cloudy day."

"Girl you're quoting the Temptations. You're in love."

Every time Kya fell in love with a man, she incorporated lyrics to famous love songs in her everyday conversations and it was hilarious.

"What's his name, Kya?"

Kya paused.

"Hello? Kya are you there?"

"Yes, I'm here."

"Alright. What's his name?" I asked, taking a sip of

lemon-infused water.

"Alfonso."

I spit water all over my desk.

"Kya. Wait. Not Alfonso Brooks."

"Yes, but Faith, please hear me out."

"Alfonso is my ex! Why on God's green earth do I need to hear you out? He's a loser, Kya. And you're my best friend. Dating your best friend's ex is against the rules. You know that!"

"Faith, please. You've got to listen to me."

"That's why it took you so long to tell me about him. You were seeing him behind my back!"

"Faith that's not fair. You're married now. You and Alfonso were together years ago."

"We had sex Kya. Is that what you want? My leftovers? My sloppy seconds?"

"That was harsh."

"No, what's harsh is you dating a guy who caused me so much grief. It was you who told me to dump him and go on that cruise without him."

"And on that cruise, you met Blaise. Your husband."

"That's not the point."

"Faith will you please hear me out?"

I tapped my acrylics on the desk as Kya quickly offered me an explanation.

"First of all, Alfonso looks entirely different and I didn't recognize him when I saw him in the store."

"How different does he look?"

"Well for starters, he doesn't have cornrows

17

anymore. He has a low cut fade now. Secondly, he's gained probably fifty pounds. When you dated him, he was chiseled. He's not anymore."

"Ok well when you found him on social media, didn't that give you a clue? You didn't see old pictures of him and me together on his page?"

"No, because he deleted all of his past accounts. He said he just returned to social media within the last six months."

"What's his name on social media?" I pulled up my social media account on the computer.

"He goes by his middle name now. Jude Brooks."

I went to Alfonso's page and was shocked by how different he looked. I hardly recognized him and could understand how Kya didn't either.

"How did he gain so much weight?" I asked.

"He has lupus and the medication caused his weight gain."

I paused for a beat and then said, "Ok but you look exactly the same. You mean to tell me that he didn't recognize you?"

"He said that when he first saw me in the grocery store I looked familiar but he couldn't place where he had seen me. He didn't realize who I was until after he saw my social media."

"Then he should've said something," I interjected.

"He didn't know how to tell me who he was at first and figured he would just remain my friend. But as time passed and we talked more, our feelings for each other just grew. When he invited me to lunch for the first time, he told me who he was and I was shocked, but then I got over it. He's literally a different person now, Faith. Being diagnosed with Lupus was scary for him, so he started going to church. He gave his life to God and enrolled in seminary. He's different. It's like that Bible verse that says, 'My whole life has changed since you came in'..."

I rolled my eyes. "That's a song by Ginuwine, Kya."

"Oh. Well, you know what I mean. He's different now that he's saved. He even asked if he should talk to you."

"Talk to me for what?"

"He just doesn't want you to think he's being disrespectful by dating me. I told him that it wouldn't be necessary to talk to you because I knew that you would be understanding when I explained everything to you. I guess I was wrong."

"Stop being dramatic," I quipped. "And excuse me if I'm not bursting at the seams to congratulate you on being with my ex."

"Don't look at it as me being with your ex--"

"But that's exactly what this is, Kya. Have you guys had sex?"

"Didn't you hear me say that he's a youth pastor now?"

"That's doesn't mean anything these days. Youth pastors have sex too and you didn't answer my question. Did you guys have sex?"

"No Faith. Jude is celibate."

"Well I don't know about this *Jude* guy, but Alfonso was a mess. Him going by his middle name doesn't mean he's changed, Kya. I don't believe you fell for this."

"And I don't believe you're not over your ex."

"Of course I'm over that loser--"

"Then what's the problem? You're happily married now and expecting your first child. Alfo..excuse me, Jude is completely different now and I'm falling in love with him. Why can't you be happy for me?"

"Because it's weird and it's against best friend code. When you found out that he was Alfonso, that should've been the end of it. Period."

"Wow. I never thought you were that type," Kya sighed.

"What type?"

"The type of friend who is so busy enjoying her happiness that she can't enjoy the happiness of anyone else. I guess you're the only one who deserves to experience true love right?"

My blood was beginning to boil. "Ok, what you're *not* going to do is accuse me of being anything but an amazing friend. Who was there for you during your last heartbreak? Who came to the club in the middle of the night and held your hair back while you hovered over the toilet puking because you were sloppy drunk? And from there who took you home, cleaned you up, and tucked you in? That was me. Because I'm that ride or die friend who knows how to stay loyal. Too bad you're not the same."

My hands were trembling as I hung up the phone. I didn't want to hear anything Kya had to say and I couldn't believe that she was actually trying to justify her new relationship with Alfonso.

That night I sat up in bed replaying the entire conversation with Blaise.

"Wait. So you mean to tell me that Kya is with the dude who was on the cruise with you? The guy who was in your room that morning I was trying to find you?"

"Yes. Can you believe it?"

"That guy was a jerk."

"I know," I said, clapping my hands together. "I can't believe she's being so stupid."

"Did she say he treats her better than he treated you?"

"She claims that he's completely changed and that he's saved now."

"Oh well, that's a good sign."

I glared at Blaise. "No, it isn't. I don't care if he's transformed himself into the Apostle Paul, I don't want Kya with him."

"So then this has nothing to do with him possibly breaking her heart."

"Of course it does," I stammered. "I don't want to see Kya get hurt again."

Blaise pursed his lips. "But what if he never breaks her heart?"

"Trust me. He will."

"But what if he doesn't."

"Blaise," I said, annoyed. "Whose side are you on?"

"I'm on your side, and you should be on the side that wants to see Kya happy."

"I *am* on that side. But she'll never be happy with Alfonso."

"Why? Because you weren't?"

"I can't believe you don't understand this," I said, rolling my eyes.

My phone rang and I sighed when I saw who it was. "Hello?"

"Hi, Faith. It's Sheila."

"Hi, Sheila."

"How are you liking Atlanta?" she asked.

"I'm liking it a lot."

"That's nice."

"Sheila, can I call you back? You kinda caught me at a bad time."

"Oh ok. I'm sorry." Sheila seemed a bit embarrassed. "Can we talk tomorrow?"

"That may work."

I hung up the phone and noticed Blaise giving me the side-eye.

"What?" I asked.

"You were awfully dismissive of your mother, just now. I know this is hard, but at least she's trying."

"She's not my mother, Blaise."

"Ok, I get your point, but she at least gave birth to you so, in that sense, she's your mother."

"False," I snapped. "She's an egg donor. A mother is supposed to kiss boo-boos, and rock you to sleep at night. A mother is supposed to be nurturing and caring and…" My voice trailed off as tears filled my eyes.

"Baby, please don't cry," Blaise said. "I'm sorry. You're right. She wasn't a mother to you."

"And it just hit me," I sniffed. "I've never had a mother. The woman I call mom is great now that she's made her peace with God and forgiven Daddy for the affair, but growing up she wasn't nurturing to me at all. And I don't even really blame her for that."

"Faith, please don't get yourself worked up--"

"If I've never known the true love of a mother, how can I expect to *give* motherly love?"

Blaise took a kleenex and wiped my face.

"You are going to be a great mother because you're a great wife, you're a great daughter, a great friend, and sister. You're a wonderful person, Faith and there is no doubt in my mind that our little one is going to be head over heels in love with you, just as much as I am."

I wiped my face and sniffed. "Thanks, Blaise."

Blaise was so sure of his words, but I wasn't so sure that he was right.

CHAPTER 5

*S*heila looked over her shoulder as she knocked on the door like a woodpecker.

A woman who reeked of bourbon swung the door open, but when she saw Sheila she closed it just to the point of being cracked. Her deep brown eyes were droopy, her hair was the color of dirty water, and her skin was as supple as crate paper.

"Not tonight Sheila," she slurred.

Sheila pushed the door open almost knocking the frail woman to the ground. She slammed the door as one cat hissed in the distance, while two others purred at Sheila's feet. The lights were dim in the one-bedroom apartment and the steady dripping of the leaky kitchen faucet sounded like despair. Sheets covered the windows and the stench of mothballs was inescapable.

"Please Ms. Henrietta. I beg of you," Sheila pleaded.

Miss Henrietta adjusted her tattered housecoat and said, "You're always beggin' of me, and I'm sick of it. You're just like my daughter, God rest her soul, but I'm tired of bailin' you out."

"You're not bailing me out, you're saving my life. And think back to what your daughter's last request was before she died. What did you promise her?"

"I know what I promised her."

"Say it," Sheila groaned.

"I promised to take care of her best friend."

"Ok then. This is the last night," Sheila said, locking the deadbolt lock and fastening the chain lock on the top of the door.

"Are you still running from that man?"

"Does it even matter?"

"Heck yeah it matters, 'cuz when you run from him, he goes lookin' fer ya, and I don't want no trouble."

"Well all of my troubles could be over in just a few days," Sheila sighed.

"How you figure that?"

"I found my daughter."

Ms. Henrietta gasped. "Did ya really?"

"Yep," Sheila replied. "And get this. She's rich."

Ms. Henrietta burst into laughter. "Girl you must've gone back to suckin' on that bottle, 'cuz I know you don't have a rich daughter."

"I do. She's beautiful *and* she has a handsome husband. They just moved to Atlanta and if my plan comes together like I think it will, they're gonna fly me down there to live and Kevin won't be able to find me."

"Well I hope it works out for ya kid," Ms. Henrietta said, taking a drink.

Sheila's mouth dropped open in astonishment as the flashing light of the television caught their attention. It was a preview for the next episode of Hollywood Gram. The words "Celebrity Sighting" appeared on the screen, followed by a brief clip of Blaise and Faith walking out of an Atlanta restaurant.

"I think that's my daughter and her husband," Sheila said, squinting.

"No way," Ms. Henrietta said.

"Wait let me look closer," Sheila said, walking right up to the television. "My goodness, it's them."

A young blonde-haired reporter appeared on the screen holding a mic and said,

"Jazz pianist Blaise Hawthorne was spotted leaving The Capital Grill restaurant in Atlanta with his new wife. We caught up with him to ask him about marriage."

Sheila and Miss Henrietta stood frozen staring at the television as the young blonde-haired reporter shouted, "Blaise! How is married life treating you?"

Blaise smiled and motioned his hand toward Faith. "I mean look at her," he said with a grin. "And she's just as beautiful on the inside."

The reporter gushed and said, "Sounds like you're loving it."

"There are no words to describe it. I've never been happier." Faith flashed an awkward smile, as they scurried along away from the cameras.

Ms. Henrietta pushed her glasses up the bridge of her nose and squinted at the television.

"I can tell that's yer daughter because she looks just like you."

"Aww thanks, Ms. Hen," Sheila said.

"She's a whole lot prettier though," Ms. Henrietta cackled.

Sheila rolled her eyes.

"If you were still drinkin' I'd raise my glass to ya. Talk about rags to riches. From the shelter to the high life, who woulda thunk it. Proud of ya kid."

"Thanks Ms. Hen," Sheila said. "When I move to Atlanta I'm going to finally live the high life."

CHAPTER 6

BLAISE

I sat at my grand piano, closed my eyes and tickled the ivories until the stress hovering over me began to dissipate. This husband gig was much harder than I ever dreamed. I played some Stevie Wonder and sang along.

"For so long, for this night I prayed...that a star...would guide you my way..."

I heard footsteps and looked up. Faith was standing there in one of my hoodies and a pair of yoga pants. Her hair was pulled up into a cluster of curls that sat atop her head and tears were streaming down her face. I wanted to say, *what now?*

But instead, I said, "Faith what's wrong, baby?"

"I don't know what to do. Sheila just called and asked if she could come to Atlanta and stay here for a while. She said she wants to build a relationship with me."

"That's great baby," I replied.

"Is it, Blaise?" Faith asked, plopping down on the sofa.

"Of course it is," I replied. "Your mother is showing you how remorseful she is for not having a relationship with you. She's finally reaching out after all these years and I think it's great."

"What if she has an ulterior motive? I don't even know who she is, or if I can trust her."

"What would her ulterior motive be?"

"Blaise you're loaded."

"But she doesn't know that."

"All it would take is her Googling your name to know."

"But we've been praying about God mending your broken heart over not knowing your birth mother, and now she shows up out of the blue. Maybe this is an answer to prayer."

Faith sighed and rolled her eyes.

"What's that for?" I asked.

"You seeing the world through your rose-colored glasses is annoying. And I know it's not your fault that you came from an amazing family, but I *do* think that it's preventing you from understanding what I'm going through."

"Faith I'm just--"

"And if she comes here will she stay until the baby is born? Do I even want her around my baby?"

"Our baby," I corrected.

Faith ignored my correction and continued lamenting. "I just don't know what to do." She paused for a beat and said, "Maybe I'll tell her that she should just stay in Texas, and I'll go back and visit frequently. We can establish somewhat of a relationship that way."

"Or you could just extend grace and let her move to Atlanta."

"And where would she stay?"

"At my house in Tybee Island."

"You would let her stay there? For free?"

"I don't need her money, Faith."

"I know, but it's just the principal of the matter. She abandons me for my entire life and now all of a sudden she's back and I'm supposed to roll out the red carpet?"

"What would Jesus do?" I said with a smile.

Faith sucked her teeth. "He would be more understanding of his wife."

And that's when I lost it.

"Fine, do whatever you want," I snapped. "I don't even know why you asked for my advice."

Faith stormed out of the room, went into the bathroom down the hall and slammed the door.

I sat at the piano in silence until I heard Faith shriek.

"Faith? You alright? What is it?" I called out.

I rushed to the bathroom as Faith was walking out with fresh tears in her eyes.

"What is it?" I asked.

"I'm bleeding."

My heart sank. On top of everything were we losing the baby?

CHAPTER 7

FAITH

"*H*ello, Dr. Woods' answering service," the secretary recited.

The words shot out of my mouth like a cannon.

"Yes, I just went to the bathroom, and there was blood in the toilet."

"Ok, are you expecting?"

"Yes, ma'am."

"Alright, and how many weeks are you?"

"About seven weeks."

"The office opens in the morning at eight. You can call at that time and make an appointment to come in."

"That's it? What do I do in the meantime?"

"Get some rest and do your best not to stress over this. I know it's easier said than done."

"There has to be something else I can do."

"If you begin cramping and bleeding profusely you should go to the Emergency Room immediately."

When I got off the phone with the receptionist Blaise said, "So?"

"There's nothing we can do, but just wait and hope that I don't start cramping and bleeding profusely. The doctor's office opens at eight and I can call in to make an appointment at that time."

"Wow," was all Blaise said and it annoyed me. Everything annoyed me.

It felt like Blaise read my mind because he said, "We need to pray."

We held hands as Blaise poured out his heart to God.

"Help us, Father. We're scared and we just want our baby to be pk. And because of that, we dedicate this baby to you right now, in Jesus' name. We don't know your plans for this child, but we *do* know that your plan is best. Help us to take comfort in your sovereignty right now. Please help us to be calm during this time and help us to get along. Give us wisdom about how to handle Sheila. And Lord if she doesn't know you as her Savior, please guide her to yourself. We thank you and we love you, Father. In Jesus' name, I pray, Amen."

Nothing had changed, but I could tell Blaise was at peace. Oh, how I longed for that peace to come over me.

CHAPTER 8

BLAISE

*T*held my breath as the doctor squirted gel on Faith's stomach and then guided the doppler along her abdomen in hopes of hearing a heartbeat.

Faith squeezed my hand and a single tear raced down her cheek.

No heartbeat.

Judging from the concerned expression on Dr. Woods's face I assumed the worst. And then out of nowhere, we heard it. The swift and muffled sound of a heart beating rapidly and in precision.

Faith let out a sigh and began sobbing.

"That's a strong heartbeat," Dr. Woods said. "One hundred and eighty beats a minute."

"So the baby's alright?" I asked.

"We'll do a blood test to monitor Faith's HCG

levels, but in the meantime, that strong heartbeat is a good sign."

"Thank you, Jesus," Faith cried.

"But why was she bleeding in the first place doc?" I asked.

"There are several variables to be considered when determining why a woman in her first trimester would begin spotting. Did you have intercourse within twenty-four hours of the spotting?"

"No," Faith responded.

I clenched my teeth. It had been too long since I had been intimate with my wife. Between her easing back into work, stressing over her biological mother, and being utterly exhausted all the time, the last thing on her mind was intimacy with me. I longed to make love to my wife, but at the risk of sounding like an insensitive jerk, I kept my feelings to myself.

"Let's do a blood test and we'll go from there," Dr. Woods said. "If you have high HCG levels we won't worry about it. Some women experience breakthrough bleeding early on in their pregnancy and still go on to deliver a healthy baby."

As she wiped the gel off of Faith's belly and tossed her latex gloves into the trash, Dr. Woods said,

"You can go ahead and get dressed, Faith. When you are finished you can go to the lab to have the nurse draw your blood."

"Ok and when will we get the results of the blood test?"

"Within twenty-four hours."

"Thank you so much doctor," Faith said.

"Sure thing. Have a great day guys." Dr. Woods left the room and Faith let out a huge sigh of relief.

"Blaise, did you hear that little heartbeat?"

"I sure did baby," I said, nuzzling her neck. "God is good."

CHAPTER 9

I sank deeper into the warm bubbles in the jacuzzi tub. Blaise had been reading every pregnancy book known to man and wouldn't let me take a hot bath.

"You can't take a hot bath when you're pregnant," he'd said.

So every time I took a bath he insisted on testing the water to make sure it wasn't too hot. I chuckled to myself as I took a sip of my preferred drink of choice these days. Sparkling cider. I drank it every day. Several times a day. I guess that meant it was a craving. In the distance, I could hear Blaise playing the piano. That seemed to be his new hobby and I wondered if he missed being on the road. In the meantime, I fantasized about hearing our baby's heartbeat. It was the single most beautiful moment I had ever experienced. It was an incredible reminder of God's sovereignty and grace in my life.

My cell phone rang and I winced when I saw who was calling. I dried my hands on a nearby towel and answered the phone.

"Hello, Sheila."

"Hi, Faith. How are you doing?"

"I'm fine Sheila, and yourself?"

"I'm good. Well, maybe not so good. There's been a lot weighing on me and I felt the need to say something to you."

I sat up in the jacuzzi, pressing the phone to my ear, not knowing whether to be annoyed, apprehensive or both at the same time. Sheila continued with a tremor in her voice.

"I'm sorry Faith. I'm sorry that I wasn't a mother to you. I'm sorry that you were probably so confused during your childhood. I'm just so sorry, but I was young and foolish at the time."

Anger and frustration stole my voice. Sheila continued.

"I knew that I wouldn't be able to raise you by myself. I was struggling with alcoholism and substance abuse and that lasted for a really long time. I'm so much better now though. Five hundred and seventy-three days clean and sober."

I offered a very sanitized, "Congratulations."

"Thank you, Faith. I just want you to please forgive

me and give me the opportunity to get to know you. To offer you any kind of support."

A sarcastic laugh escaped my lips and against my better judgment, I said what I'd been thinking deep down inside all along. "You want to offer me any kind of support? Now? I needed your support when I was seven years old. That's when I noticed that the woman who I thought was my mother wouldn't hold me as long in her embrace like she held my siblings. I noticed it. When she held my brothers and sister her love lingered. She relished in their laughter. She was proud of their stick figure drawings. But everything I did was cherished like a vain afterthought."

Silence.

"Do you know what Easter was like for me, Sheila? The woman who I thought was my mother would put pretty ribbons in my sister's hair. But I got no ribbons and my daddy didn't notice, because he was too busy trying to make up for his transgressions. Too busy trying to get his wife to forget about his sins. But how could she? I was the fruit of his tainted harvest. I was a walking breathing mistake. A constant reminder of brokenness. Pardon me if I'm not bursting at the seams to forgive you right now."

"Faith, please give me another chance. If I could physically show you my heart, you'd see the regret that I have. Please let me make it up to you."

"You can't make it up, Sheila!" I cried. "You would

have to go back in time and decide to be my mother instead of abandoning me. You can't do that."

"Faith please."

Anger swelled up around my heart and hardened it. I hung up the phone without saying goodbye.

CHAPTER 10

FAITH

*C*onviction swept over me as Pastor Albright read the scripture text. "Then Peter came to Jesus and asked, 'Lord, how many times shall I forgive my brother or sister who sins against me? Up to seven times?'

Jesus answered, "I tell you, not seven times, but seventy-seven times. Therefore, the kingdom of heaven is like a king who wanted to settle accounts with his servants. As he began the settlement, a man who owed him ten thousand bags of gold was brought to him. Since he was not able to pay, the master ordered that he and his wife and his children and all that he had be sold to repay the debt.

At this, the servant fell on his knees before him. 'Be patient with me,' he begged, 'and I will pay back everything. The servant's master took pity on him, canceled the debt and let him go.

But when that servant went out, he found one of his fellow servants who owed him a hundred silver coins. He grabbed him and began to choke him. 'Pay back what you owe me!' he demanded.

His fellow servant fell to his knees and begged him, 'Be patient with me, and I will pay it back.' But he refused. Instead, he went off and had the man thrown into prison until he could pay the debt. When the other servants saw what had happened, they were outraged and went and told their master everything that had happened.

Then the master called the servant in. 'You wicked servant,' he said, 'I canceled all that debt of yours because you begged me to. Shouldn't you have had mercy on your fellow servant just as I had on you?' In anger, his master handed him over to the jailers to be tortured, until he should pay back all he owed.

This is how my heavenly Father will treat each of you unless you forgive your brother or sister from your heart."

I couldn't tell if I was on the verge of losing my breakfast because of the pregnancy or because of the scripture passage that Pastor Albright had just read. I had never heard it before, but it hit me right between the eyes.

"It's hard to forgive isn't it?" Pastor Albright asked.

The congregation answered in the form of raised hands and a variety of Amens as the pastor continued.

"Oh but saints, nothing was harder than the sacrifice Jesus made on that hill called Calvary. He took on the sins of the entire world and actually became sin that we all might have life. So when you read this parable do you recognize yourself? It's easy to say that the man who wouldn't forgive is so terrible. After all, he'd been forgiven of a huge debt, but wouldn't forgive the guy who owed him a small debt. Saints, I'm here to tell you that when we don't forgive, we *are* that man. And in the latter part of the passage, it says that he was taken away to be tortured until he could repay the great debt that he owed. Brothers and sisters if you don't forgive, God will allow you the same torture and I'm not talking about physical torture. I'm talking about the mental anguish that comes when you refuse to demonstrate forgiveness. Think about someone you know who's holding a grudge and ask yourself, is that person happy? Do they have a cheery disposition or are they always spewing venom? It's because deep down inside that person is tortured."

It felt as if an actual spotlight was shining on me. Blaise wrapped his arm around me and whispered, "You alright baby? You look sick."

"I'm fine. I just need some water."

A kind woman in front of me turned around and handed me an unopened bottle of water.

"Here you go, sweetheart. I couldn't help but hear you say that you needed some water. And my name is Minnie, by the way."

The woman looked to be the same age as Sheila and

she had kindness in her eyes.

"Thank you, Miss Minnie," I replied.

I took a sip of the water, doing my best to ignore Blaise's concerned gaze.

After church as Blaise was talking to an usher about sports, I slipped away to talk to Pastor Albright.

"How are you doing Sister Faith?"

"Pastor I need some advice." I spent the next ten minutes telling Pastor Albright about my situation. I needed to hear from someone who wasn't directly tied to my issues.

"First of all Faith, you can't forgive in your own strength and that's why this feels so impossible. True forgiveness can only come through the supernatural work of the Holy Spirit."

"Ok, so after I'm able to forgive, do I let my biological mother back into my life? I don't even know what kind of person she is now."

"I can't give you all of the answers sis. But the good news is that God has all of the answers and He won't steer you wrong."

"How do I get the answers from God?" I asked, puzzled.

"Through prayer," Pastor Albright replied. "Go to the Lord in prayer. Talk to him the same way you're talking to me. He'll give you the exact answers that you need."

That evening over dinner, I told Blaise about my conversation with Pastor Albright.

Blaise took a sip of sweet tea and said, "I remember when Sugar didn't know what to do, she would fast and pray until God gave her the answer."

"Blaise, I'm pregnant. I can't fast right now."

"You don't have to fast from food. You can fast from anything that's a distraction to you."

"I guess I *am* on social media quite a bit."

"There you go," Blaise said. "Take a break from all social media until God gives you the answer. I'll do it with you."

Once again I was reminded how blessed I was to have a husband like Blaise. I watched him for a moment as he devoured the steak and mashed potatoes that I had prepared for dinner. Just casually sitting at the table in his blue muscle shirt and jogging shorts, he looked as delicious as the steak. He looked up and noticed my eyes on him.

"What?" he asked. "Do I have some food on my face or something?"

"No," I sighed, leaning in for a kiss.

"What's that for?" Blaise asked, grinning like a Cheshire cat.

"It's for being an amazingly patient husband. Now let's go upstairs so I can give you a proper thank you."

"Girl you ain't said nothing but a word," Blaise howled.

We spent the rest of the day loving on each other, praying and dreaming about the future. I didn't know what was in store, but I was determined to trust God every step of the way.

CHAPTER 11

"*H*elp me!"

I jumped up, startled by the screams.

"Help me, please!" the voice called out again.

I began running toward the voice, determined to help whoever it was. As I ran closer to the voice I began smelling smoke. There were flames in the distance as the screams became more intense.

"Faith! Please help me, daughter!"

"Mom!" I called out. "I'm coming to save you!"

I finally reached my mother. She was slumped over in a corner and her clothes were on fire. I somehow managed to grab her and pull her up without being consumed by the flames. When she looked up at me, I gasped. It was Sheila.

"You're the only one who can save me, Faith! I need to be saved!"

"I can't save you!" I cried.

"But you know the one who can! Show me the way! Please!"

I jumped up out of bed, drenched in sweat and out of breath as if I had been running a marathon through the night.

Blaise opened his eyes and sat up as soon as he saw me.

"Faith, baby what's wrong?"

"I just had a nightmare about Sheila."

"What was the nightmare about?" Blaise asked.

"Sheila was on fire and begging me to save her." I paused for a moment as one hundred thoughts raced through my mind. "At the end of the day, Sheila needs the Lord, and maybe God wants to use me to bring her to him."

"Looks like we've got our answer," Blaise said.

With fear in my heart, I dialed Sheila's number. It was three in the morning, but I didn't care and I knew she wouldn't either.

"Hello?" her groggy voice croaked.

My hands trembled as I spoke three words that set me free.

"I forgive you."

CHAPTER 12

*N*o matter how old I got, I never tired of going home to my parents.

"Come on in Bebe," Mama said, reaching up to hug my neck. "Honey, Bebe is here!"

Pops came downstairs and said, "How's the Father-to-be?"

But when he saw my facial expression, his tone became less jovial.

"What's wrong son?" Mama asked. "Come on in the living room and let's talk."

I sat down with my parents and told them about Sheila.

"Well it's good that Faith decided to forgive her," Mama said.

"I know," I said. "And as much as I was on board with Sheila moving to Atlanta, now I'm having second thoughts. I just don't want Faith to become overly stressed. Can't stress affect the baby?"

"That's where you come in son," Pops said. "Be her peace. Comfort her whenever you can. This won't be an easy transition, but with God all things are possible. I'm proud of Faith."

"I am too." I paused for a moment and said, "I know what I'm about to say isn't right, but at the risk of sounding judgmental, I can't help but think about how much easier life would be right now if Faith's dad had never cheated, and if she was his daughter by his wife. I just don't understand adultery. If you're not happy in your marriage, then end it, but don't cheat." I shook my head and took note of my parent's body language. Mama and Pops exchanged glances and held hands.

"Why are you two so quiet?" I asked.

"Bebe, our family isn't perfect," Mama said.

"What are you guys talking about?" I asked. "I know we're not perfect, but we're not dysfunctional like Faith's family."

"Not one family is better than another, Bebe. Always remember that," Pops said.

I raised an eyebrow. "What are you guys talking about?"

Mama stood up and said, "You guys want anything to drink? I'm a bit parched."

"Honey, can you get me some of that fresh-squeezed lemonade that you made last night?" Pops asked.

I began to salivate at the thought of tasting my mother's lemonade. She made it fresh-squeezed with honey and it was the best lemonade around. "Can I have a cup too, Mama?"

"Of course." Mama stood up, running her slender fingers through her salt and pepper gray curls and disappeared into the kitchen while Pops and I continued in conversation.

"Now what were you saying, Pops?"

"I was basically reminding you that no family is perfect. Our family has had our issues too."

"Well sure, we're not perfect, but we've never dealt with anything like the Caldwells have."

"Your mother and I have faced infidelity in our marriage, Bebe. And no it didn't result in an unwanted pregnancy, but it was hell and it nearly ended our marriage. I'm not proud of that time in our lives at all."

I felt like a little kid who had just discovered that Santa Claus wasn't real. I knew that my parents weren't perfect, but hearing that my father had cheated on my mother tore a hole in my heart. How could he do that to her? My mother was an angel.

Mama walked back into the living room smiling and holding a tray with three glasses of lemonade. When she looked up and saw my facial expression her smile vanished.

"What's wrong?"

"I told Bebe that we've had to heal from infidelity as well."

"Oh, Bebe," Mama said.

"It's alright," I said. I guzzled down the glass of lemonade and stood to my feet. "I'm actually going to go. I told Faith I'd meet her for lunch."

"But it's only ten o'clock," Pops said.

"I know, but I've got a few errands to run first."

I headed for the door and paused for a moment to look at the picture of my parents hanging on the wall. They seemed like they had always been happy. It hurt me to know that I was wrong.

Right before I walked out of the door, Pops put a firm hand on my shoulder and said, "When you're ready to talk, let me know alright son?"

Without turning around to face him I said, "Sure thing, Pops." And headed out the door.

For the first time in my life, my father, my hero had let me down.

y hands were so sweaty that the phone nearly dropped from my grasp. Blaise stood behind me with his hands on my shoulders.

"It's going to be ok baby," he whispered. "Take a deep breath."

I looked around Blaise's living room at the cathedral ceiling, the fine art on the walls, the white leather sofa and loveseat, and the Persian rug sitting atop the hardwood floor. I had become accustomed to this lavish lifestyle and wondered how Sheila would adjust to it.

Finally, on the third ring, she answered.

"Hello?"

"Hi Sheila, it's Faith."

"Hi, Faith. Thanks so much for calling me again."

"No problem. I know that our last conversation was

brief, but I just wanted to extend an invitation for you to come to Atlanta."

I could hear Sheila clap her hands.

"Do you really mean it? You want me to come?"

"I do," I said. "I think it will be good for both of us."

"I'm as happy as a lark," Sheila exclaimed. "Do I need to get a bus pass?"

"No," I chuckled. "We'll fly you here."

"Wow. I've never been on a plane before."

I talked over the details with Sheila and agreed that we would fly her to Atlanta next week.

"I can hardly wait," Sheila exclaimed.

When I hung up the phone Blaise said, "Mrs. Hawthorne, I am very proud of you."

"Nothing but God," I replied. "I'm just realizing that this whole thing is so much bigger than me."

"So true," Blaise agreed.

Blaise was silent for a moment and when I looked up at him he had a goofy grin on his face.

"What?" I asked.

"Look at your belly," Blaise said. "It's starting to poke out a little."

I rushed over to the mirror in the foyer, lifted my shirt and looked sideways at my stomach. I rubbed it back and forth and marveled at how firm it was.

"Our baby is in there Blaise."

Blaise wrapped his arms around my waist and kissed my belly. "Soon it will be time for us to find out if it's a boy or a girl, and I plan to throw the gender reveal party of the century." Blaise pulled out his phone and looked at the calendar. "Our one year anniversary is the same week as the ultrasound. You know what that means ..."

"That you're going to do entirely too much," I giggled.

"To be fair, we didn't do much for our wedding remember? Only invited close family. We said that for our one year anniversary we'd have a huge reception and invite everyone. So I'm thinking we should plan a gender reveal, slash baby shower, slash anniversary party. What do you think? We only have about a month, but if I get my party planner on it, I know she'll be able to pull it off."

"I think it's crazy, but go ahead and run with it."

Blaise scooped me up and twirled me around. "You won't regret it!"

My phone chirped and I rolled my eyes. It was a text message from Kya.

Faith it's been too long since we've talked. This is ridiculous.

I replied.

If you're still with Alfonso, we have nothing to discuss.

There was no response after that, but Blaise could see the annoyance dripping from my face.

"Was that Kya again?"

"It sure was," I groaned. "I don't know why she doesn't understand how wrong this is."

"Sounds like she's found happiness and wants to share it with her best friend."

"Happiness Blaise? She's with Alfonso. She's miles away from happiness."

"But he could have changed."

"There are those rose-colored glasses again," I sighed.

"It's not rose-colored glasses, it's just me realizing that Kya is a great friend and--"

"A great friend doesn't date your ex, Blaise."

"She didn't know he was your ex when she first caught feelings for him."

"But when she realized who he was, she should've ended it. Period."

"Faith think of what you're asking her to do. She finally finds someone who she's compatible with. He's everything she's ever wanted in a man and she's genuinely happy, but you expect her to give all of that up because of the past."

"I'm not having this discussion again."

"Fine," Blaise said. "But if you really love Kya, you'll want her to be happy."

"I *do* want her to be happy, but what I'm *not* going to do is discuss this any further."

I went upstairs and left Blaise standing in the foyer. Every time we took two steps forward, we ended up taking three steps back.

CHAPTER 14

I didn't know if it was my nerves or the baby, but I couldn't keep anything down all morning. The frustrating part was that Sheila was flying in and when I should've been on my way to the airport to pick her up with Blaise, I was on my knees, hugging the toilet.

After losing what felt like everything I'd eaten for the last two weeks, I stood up, steadied myself and brushed my teeth. I looked in the mirror at my blood-shot eyes and flushed face.

Get it together, Faith.

I took a warm shower and washed my hair. Maybe if I looked better, I'd feel better too.

Fresh out of the shower wrapped in a towel, I applied raw coconut oil to my hair and brushed it back into a braid. I couldn't believe how long my hair was getting. I dried off, moisturized my skin with baby oil, slipped on a tiffany blue maxi dress, and put a peppermint in my mouth to keep nausea at bay. A beat later my phone rang. It was Blaise.

"Hey Faith," Blaise's voice was just above a whisper.

"What's going on?" I asked, gasping.

"Ok, first of all. Calm down. And how are you feeling? Still throwing up?"

"I'm much better now. Why are you whispering?"

"Because I don't want Sheila to hear me. We stopped so she could use the bathroom, but she'll be back soon. Anyway, I just wanted to give you a heads up about Sheila..."

"What about Sheila?"

"She's back. I gotta go," Blaise whispered.

"Blaise please tell me what's going on."

"Please relax. We'll be home in about twenty minutes."

Blaise hung up and I wanted to explode. What could he have possibly been trying to give me a heads up about? I paced back and forth praying for the next twenty minutes.

"God please help me to calm down and relax. Please bless Blaise and Sheila with safety. Please work this whole situation out. Please, God."

I could hear Blaise walk in the door and playfully shout, "Honey, we're home!"

I rushed down the stairs and Sheila was standing in the living room looking around like a little kid in a coliseum. As I got closer to her my heart dropped. Half of her face was completely swollen and she had a black eye.

I tried to look pleasant, even though I was alarmed inside.

"Sheila are you alright?" I asked.

"Hi, Faith! Yes, I'm alright. I'm just so clumsy. I tripped and fell down the stairs the other day."

Sheila walked toward me with her arms outstretched. "Thank you for having me," she said, hugging my neck. "Thank you so much."

I returned the hug and Sheila lingered. She wouldn't let me go. As I was hugging her I looked up at Blaise who was standing behind Sheila.

He pointed to his eye and mouthed the words, *that's what I was trying to give you a heads up about.*

I took Sheila's hand and led her to the sofa.

"Have a seat, Sheila. Do you want anything to drink? Water, soda, juice?"

"I'll have water please," Sheila replied.

Blaise disappeared into the kitchen to retrieve a bottled water and I did my best not to stare at Sheila's wounds.

"So how was your flight?"

"It was really nice. So quick. I couldn't believe it."

Sheila's silver hair was pulled back into a tiny bun. She wore a white t-shirt with a pair of blue jeans and carried all of her belongings in grocery store plastic bags.

"Yeah, flying is the best way to travel, because of how quickly it goes."

There was a second of silence, broken by Blaise who walked in with ice-cold bottled water. "Here ya go, Sheila."

"Thanks," Sheila said with a half-smile.

"Are you hungry?" I asked. "We're going to get you settled into your place, but first we can eat if you'd like."

"That sounds great," Sheila said.

"Great," Blaise said. "What do you have a taste for?"

"I'm not picky," Sheila said. "Y'all can surprise me."

"You sure?" I asked.

"Yes ma'am," Sheila said, clutching her bags.

While Blaise left to get food, Sheila and I conversed on the sofa.

"So Sheila," I said. "Tell me a little about your upbringing."

On the inside, I was wincing. *Dumb question Faith.*

"Well," Sheila said. "I didn't have much of an upbringing. My mother worked two jobs so she was hardly ever home, and I don't know who my father is."

"I'm sorry to hear that," I replied.

"It is what it is," Sheila said. "What was your upbringing like?"

"Well," I hesitated, choosing my words carefully. "It wasn't perfect, but it wasn't terrible either. "I have two brothers that kept me busy and I spent most summers with my dad's mother."

"Ah, Granny C right?"

"Yep, that's her. Spending time with her was the best part of my childhood."

Sheila nodded with a half-smile and said, "Um Faith. I hope you know how much I appreciate this. And I plan to pull my weight to help pay for stuff. I can get a job and give you guys some of my paycheck each time I get paid."

I held my hand up. "That won't be necessary Sheila."

"But I'd like to do *something,*" Sheila said.

"Ok, I know what you can do," I replied. "Have you been to church before?"

"I think I went once."

"Just go with me to church."

Sheila's eyes grew wide. "Just one time?"

"Each week, if possible."

"Well that seems fair enough," Sheila said.

We continued chatting on the sofa until Blaise arrived with takeout from Olive Garden.

Blaise prepared Sheila's plate and looked surprised when Sheila began scarfing the food down.

"I'm going to say a blessing over the food."

"I'm sorry," Sheila said, wiping her mouth with a napkin.

"No problem at all," Blaise said, bowing his head. "Father we thank you so much for the food that is before us, we thank you for our guest who is here with us, and we ask that you would bless our fellowship. In Jesus' name, we pray, Amen."

When Sheila finished eating she fell asleep on the sofa.

I looked at Blaise and whispered, "I don't think she should stay at your place on Tybee Island."

"I was thinking the same thing," Blaise whispered.

"She needs our help, and we won't be able to keep an eye on her if she's all the way over there."

Blaise nodded his head in agreement.

That night after we got Sheila settled in, I lay in bed tossing and turning. No matter what position I laid in, I couldn't get comfortable and I couldn't get my mind to shut off.

Blaise turned over to face me.

"What's wrong Faith?"

"I can't get comfortable and my mind is racing."

"What are you thinking about? Sheila?"

"Not just Sheila. I'm thinking about the entire situation and how since my dad told me the truth, I've been so resentful of Sheila's decision to give me up. But now that I've had a chance to talk to her in-depth, I'm thankful for the decision she made. Who knows what my life would have turned out like if she *hadn't* given me up. I see now that it was for the best."

Blaise wrapped his arm around my waist and said, "All things work together…"

"Exactly," I said.

"When are we going to talk about the argument we had over Kya?" Blaise asked.

I rolled my eyes. "We may have to agree to disagree on that one because I still feel the same way."

Blaise chuckled. "That's a deal."

I leaned my head back nestled in Blaise's chest and drifted off to sleep. When I woke up, Blaise's head was next to my hip and he was talking to my stomach.

"Every good and every perfect gift comes from above. That's you, baby. You're our good and perfect gift and Daddy can't wait to meet you."

A smile spread across my lips as I drifted back to sleep.

CHAPTER 15

FAITH

The further along I got in the pregnancy, the more I absolutely dreaded work. How could something that once was so enjoyable and fulfilling now be such a chore? The original plan was that after I had the baby, I would continue to work and Blaise would stay home on daddy daycare duty, but now I wasn't so sure about that arrangement.

As I sat at my desk mulling over a report and counting down till the time I could go home, my phone rang.

Facetime request from Kya.

I sucked my teeth. What did she want? I ignored the request and kept working until she requested facetime again. I wanted to ignore it, but at the end of the day, I loved Kya and was concerned that something could be wrong.

I answered her call and saw Kya's face filled with relief.

"Faith," she said.

"Yes Kya," I said in a matter of fact tone.

"I miss you."

My pride wouldn't allow me to say that I missed her too, so I simply said, "Thanks."

"Faith this is crazy, we've never gone this long without talking."

"Are you still with Alfonso?" I asked.

"Yes, Jude and I are still together."

"Kya calling him Jude doesn't change his identity."

"But he's an entirely different person now, Faith."

"Except he isn't. He's still Alfonso Brooks. My ex-boyfriend who was selfish in every way, constantly asked me for money and hinted that the saddest thing about Granny C having Alzheimer's was the fact that she might forget how to make her famous sweet potato pies. That's the guy you're with right now."

"That's who he was back then. Faith, now he's a man of God who works full time at church. Two weeks ago one of the teens from the youth group was having a meltdown at school because his parents are getting divorced and Jude went up to the school and took that kid lunch. He prayed for him and then asked his mother if he could come by and do a devotional with him that evening. The following Sunday that teenager gave his life to Christ because of the Godly impact that

Jude had on his life. That's the man I'm in a relationship with."

"Ok well that's nice, but it doesn't change the fact that he's seen me naked. Isn't that weird to you? The man that you're head over heels for has seen your best friend naked. And I've seen him naked. We've done...things. Kya that's just too weird. I'm sorry."

"Ok, I admit that I don't care to think about that part, but we don't have to focus on that. That was a long time ago and we're all adults. It's not like Blaise has a squeaky clean past either. Need I remind you of the prostitute he slept with, who ended up working for you?"

"That is entirely different, Kya. First of all that happened several years before Blaise and I met and Blaise didn't know she was a prostitute when he slept with her. Secondly, it was just a bizarre coincidence that she ended up working for me. And I don't work there anymore. Having to constantly see her while knowing about her tryst with Blaise would be awkward."

"But the point is that you know about his past, but you don't dwell on it. As adults, we can choose what consumes us."

I pursed my lips as Kya went on.

"Faith, don't you want me to be happy? You've been *saying* that you want me to be happy for years."

"I want you to be happy with a good man."

"And I am, Faith. Jude is an amazing man who God

has used to draw me closer to Him. He prays with me, he studies the Word with me, and he encourages me. And he has never even hinted that I give myself to him sexually. He's a good man and I'm so happy. Please be happy with me too."

I sighed. "It's still weird to me, but...I guess I'm happy that you're happy."

Kya clapped her hands together and squealed. "Thanks so much, Faith!"

I shook my head. "I'm still not anxious to hear about him. Baby steps, Kya."

"I understand. But right now I don't want to talk about Jude, I want to hear about what's been going on with you!"

"Oh," I chuckled. "Girl grab some popcorn."

Kya pulled out a bag of popcorn and I cackled. "Hey I'm ready," she howled.

"Ok," I began. "So Sheila has been staying with us for a few weeks."

"Wait. She's not staying at Tybee Island?"

"No. She's emotionally unstable and needs us too much."

"Wow."

"I know. But it's actually been going well."

"How far along are you now?"

"Fifteen weeks. We find out what we're having next week, which is the same week as our one year anniversary."

"Has it been a year already?"

"I know, the time has flown by."

"So how will you guys celebrate?"

"Blaise is planning a huge gender reveal, slash one year anniversary party."

Kya's facial expression suddenly went south. "And you weren't going to invite me?"

"We weren't on good terms, Kya. And the thought of Alfonso coming is weird."

"If you had asked me not to bring Jude, I wouldn't have."

"Ok. Then I would love for you to come, Kya. I must admit that even though I was upset with you, that doesn't mean that I haven't missed you like crazy. I just don't feel comfortable having Alfonso there."

"Ok. I can agree to that," Kya said.

"Then it's settled! I'll see you next week, sis!"

I felt somewhat encouraged when I ended the face-time call with Kya. It was still weird to me that she was dating my ex, but based on everything she told me, he did indeed seem to be a changed man.

I leaned back in my office chair and felt a faint fluttering in my belly.

I couldn't dial Blaise's number fast enough.

"Hello?"

"Blaise, I just felt the baby kick!"

"Oh my goodness! You did? What did it feel like?"

"It felt kinda like a butterfly fluttering inside of my stomach. So sweet."

"Do you think I'd be able to feel it?"

"Probably not. It was so faint. But soon the kicks will be strong."

"What do you think it is? A boy or a girl?" Blaise asked.

"I'm hoping for a boy."

"It doesn't matter to me what we have," Blaise said. "I just want a healthy baby who will grow up to play the piano or the saxophone. Or both," he chortled.

I leaned back and laughed until my sides hurt. All was right with the world. For now.

CHAPTER 16

BLAISE

J was awakened by the smell of bacon and coffee wafting through the air. Faith was sleeping soundly next to me so I put my robe on and went downstairs to investigate the aroma.

In the kitchen, blasting my last jazz CD was Sheila wearing her brand new silk pajamas, complete with her fuzzy slippers and matching headscarf.

"Good morning Blaise," she said with a smile. "I know that this is a big day for y'all, so I figured I'd get up early and make a big breakfast."

"How thoughtful of you, Sheila. You didn't have to do that."

"I know, but y'all have been so good to me, letting me stay here for free, buying me a new wardrobe and taking me to church, it was the least that I could do. Isn't that what your pastor said yesterday? Do to others, what you'd want them to do for you?"

"He sure did. Look at you paying attention to the sermon and stuff," I chuckled as I put my arm around Sheila. "I'm proud of you. Are you planning to come with us to the ultrasound today?"

"Oh no, I wouldn't dream of going. That's a special moment that should be between y'all. I'll stay here and wait for you to get back with the good news."

"When we get back we won't even know what we're having."

"Well, what kind of deal is that?" Sheila asked.

"Faith and I won't find out what we're having until the party this weekend when we cut the cake. If the cake is blue inside it's a boy and if it's pink inside, it's a girl."

"Well my goodness, y'all are fancy. Either way, I'll just stay here and wait until y'all come back."

Faith yawned as she walked into the kitchen, wearing an oversized night shirt that hung below her knees. "Who cooked breakfast?"

"Sheila did," I replied.

"Aww thanks so much, Sheila."

"No problem Faith." Sheila paused for a moment and began speaking with a tremor in her voice. "Seeing you go through this process of having a baby is bringing back a lot of memories from when I was carrying you." she sniffed. "I didn't have anyone to do anything nurturing for me, so I moped around and had a pity party all the time. I didn't take care of myself at all." more sniffles. "But now, I look at you and how wonderful you are and I can't help but think, I was carrying all this greatness in my womb? I should've cherished every single second because I was getting ready to give birth to a queen."

Tears streamed down Faith's face as she hugged Sheila. "Thank you so much for saying that."

I walked over and put my arms around both Faith and Sheila and said, "Group hug." The ladies laughed and my heart swelled with joy. God was answering our prayers with Sheila and her relationship with Faith was actually starting to be strengthened.

At the doctor's office, it felt like an eternity before they called Faith's name. When they finally did, we followed the nurse to the examination room like two teenagers on our way to ride a rollercoaster. It was the most exciting moment in our lives.

Dr. Woods walked in with her hair pulled up into an afro puff and said, "Alrighty Faith and Blaise, my favorite couple."

"Stop it," I said. "You probably say that to all the couples."

Dr. Woods winked and said, "You're right. But I do love you guys though."

Faith leaned back on the table and held my hand while Dr. Woods dimmed the lights.

"Alright," she said. "You guys ready to see your baby?"

"We're ready," I said.

Dr. Woods pressed the monitor against the jelly on

Faith's abdomen and there was our peanut, who had grown much bigger than a peanut. He or she was bouncing around and I thought my heart was going to literally burst with pride. Faith and I exchanged happy glances and then I looked at Dr. Woods' face. She wasn't smiling. She didn't look joyful. Instead, she was frowning and concern was etched across her face.

"Everything ok doc?" I asked.

"Let me take a closer look," was all that Dr. Woods said. She magnified the picture on the screen and focused on what looked to be the baby's head.

"What's going on Dr.?" Faith asked.

Dr. Woods pointed to the ultrasound screen in front of us. "This here is your baby's brain. And this area that's shaded in is where his or her cerebellum should be."

Faith gasped. "The baby doesn't have a cerebellum?"

"No. I'm so sorry Faith. And I'm even more sorry to tell you that that's not the most concerning part."

My heart pounded harder with each word that Dr. Woods spoke, to the point that I started to feel dizzy.

"The most concerning part is that your baby also has a mass on the brain. Now there are recorded accounts of babies who have been born without their cerebellum and they went on to live a fairly decent life with a few side effects, but that's extremely rare. The problem in your baby's case is that the mass, coupled with the fact that the cerebellum is missing, is the perfect storm."

With tears streaming down my face, I said, "So in layman's terms can you tell us what this means?"

It means that your baby probably won't live for longer than about thirty minutes after birth.

Faith burst into tears. I got on my knees next to the table where she lay and held her while she shook with grief.

Keep it together Blaise. You have to be strong for her.

Tears streamed down my cheeks, but I didn't make a sound. As much as I was hurting I couldn't imagine what Faith was feeling, actually carrying the baby within her, knowing that his or her chances for survival outside of the womb were minuscule.

I swallowed hard and managed to speak without breaking down.

"Dr. Woods I've heard that sometimes babies can have surgery in utero. Is there any way that could be an option for our baby?"

Dr. Woods looked physically pained to respond. "I'm so sorry, but for the location of the mass, there's just no way to perform the surgery. It would be too dangerous and the baby would more than likely die instantly."

"So what you're saying is that there's no hope for our baby? There's nothing we can do?" I asked, wiping the tears from my face.

Dr. Woods looked me square in the eyes as I held Faith who was still sobbing.

"Blaise, as a medical professional who's been in this

field for over twenty years, I've learned not to say that a situation has no hope. There are medical miracles that occur every day. What I will say is that according to the natural laws of medical science your baby doesn't have a good chance of survival outside of the womb. Does that mean that it's impossible for him or her to survive? No. Ultimately that's up to the man upstairs."

"And we don't call him the man upstairs, doc. We call him Jesus Christ, Son of the living God."

Dr. Woods smiled. "I stand corrected."

"We appreciate your time Doctor," I said. "Were you still able to identify the sex of the baby?"

"I sure did."

Dr. Woods wrote something down on a piece of paper and sealed it in an envelope.

"Inside this envelope is the sex of your baby."

"Thank you, Dr. Woods."

Dr. Woods left the room and Faith was still in the same position lying on the table in tears.

"Faith, baby. It's going to be alright. Come on. Sit up."

Faith sat up and fell on my chest in tears. I held her and did my best to be strong for her, but could hold it in no longer. We held each other and wept.

I finally gathered myself enough to speak. "We need to be strong for the baby, Faith. My mother told me that he or she can feel what you feel. We don't want stress on the baby."

Faith didn't speak a word, but she nodded her head in agreement.

Silence accompanied us on the ride home. When we walked into the house Sheila greeted us with exuberance.

"Well tell me all about that big ba--" her voice cut off when she saw our faces. "Oh my goodness, what happened?"

Faith trudged up the stairs without speaking, while I explained everything to Sheila.

Sheila covered her mouth while the tears fell free. "Blaise I am so incredibly sorry."

"It's alright, Sheila. I'm going to go upstairs and check on Faith."

I could hear Faith before I got up the stairs. She was weeping deep from her belly in a way that I'd never heard anyone weep before. When I opened the bedroom door she was lying on the bed screaming.

I lifted her up and held her like a baby in my arms. "Faith, baby please calm down. You're going to make yourself sick. Please."

Tiny beads of sweat framed her brow. I turned the ceiling fan on and rocked her back and forth until she drifted off to sleep. She was exhausted from crying.

I knelt at her side praying with my hand on her stomach for the entire hour that she slept. I prayed and cried, pouring out my heart to God. I told God I was scared, I told him I was angry, but most importantly I pleaded with God for a miracle.

As Faith's swollen eyelids began to flutter, I felt a sense of peace. Not because I knew that our baby would survive, but because I knew that God could be trusted.

"My head is killing me," Faith said.

"I can go get you some Tylenol."

I returned with a glass of water and two Tylenol. After Faith took the medicine, she said, "Have you started letting people know that the gender reveal party will be canceled?"

"Why would we cancel it?" I asked.

"Blaise come on. Of course, we're going to cancel it."

"Faith the point of the party on Saturday is to celebrate life while finding out what we're having as well as to celebrate the year of marriage that God has blessed us with. I see no reason to cancel all of that."

"Blaise I'm not going to plaster a smile on my face and act like everything is ok when it's not."

"Faith the whole time you were sleeping, I was praying and God really spoke to me."

"What did he say?" Faith asked.

"He said to trust him."

"That's it?" Faith asked.

"Yes. See it's easy to praise God and throw a party when we get the news that we want. But isn't he still worthy of praise when we don't get the news that we want?"

Tears started forming in my eyes as I spoke. "Faith I

trust God. I trust that whatever happens will be his will and that it will be what's best for us."

"But you're crying, Blaise," Faith sniffed.

"Trusting God doesn't mean that I won't cry. It doesn't even mean that I won't hurt. But what it *does* mean is that even with tears in my eyes I'll still rejoice in the truth that he is good and that he is to be trusted. So we're going to have that party this weekend. We're going to still celebrate and we're going to praise God because right now you're carrying our child within your womb and that is what we prayed for. We prayed for life and as of now, God has blessed us with that. He's worthy Faith."

I hung my head and cried while Faith wrapped her arms around me. We were both raw with grief, but no matter what I was determined to fully trust God and to give him praise, even with tears in my eyes.

CHAPTER 17

FAITH

*J*had already cried my makeup off twice, but the makeup artist Blaise hired was so patient with me. I sat down in her chair for a third time that morning and said, "I'm so sorry...um...um...pardon me for forgetting your name again."

"It's Onamacritus Eutsey."

I looked at her with a blank expression and Onamacritus laughed. "Just call me Rita for short."

"Got it. Thanks so much, Rita. I promise I won't cry my makeup off this time."

"And if you do," Rita said. "I've got you covered."

Rita glued my lashes back on and applied more lipstick and blush.

I looked in the mirror and was actually surprised by the results. The eye drops Rita used on my eyes made me look vibrant, and nothing like a woman who had been crying all morning. My attire, which was an all-white off the shoulder maxi dress, was everything that I had envisioned. Blaise said that stylist Rhonda Smith never disappointed and he was right. My hair was the perfect braid out, with a halo of tiffany blue and white baby's breath. I had my girl Vicky Eubanks to thank for that hairstyle and I was so thankful that she had agreed to help me out at the last minute.

I walked down the steps and the taste of aggravation filled my mouth as various vendors and caterers scurried about the kitchen preparing for all of the guests Blaise had invited.

"Excuse me, Mrs. Hawthorne, I'm Danette from Refreshing Fountains. Where do you want the chocolate fountain?"

I was glad that Danette had a cheery disposition because I was feeling just the opposite. "Danette, first of all, please call me Faith. Blaise is the one who coordinated all of this, so if you see him you can direct that question to him. He's around here somewhere."

"Ok, thank you, Mrs. Hawthorne. I mean Faith," Danette said.

As Danette scurried away there was a host of cooks in the kitchen. I was annoyed by all of the hoopla, but the aroma of the food was so amazing that I couldn't get too perturbed.

A petite woman with caramel complexion stepped up and shook my hand. "Hi Faith, I'm Bridget Rush and I'm in charge of the catering for your event. Please meet my team. This is Aquilla, Marian, Domonique,

Cassie, Mimi, and Gloria." The ladies raised their hands with smiles on their faces.

"We're happy to serve," they sang in unison.

"Thank you so much ladies," I said.

Bridgette began lifting the foil lids off of several dishes.

"Faith we've got Swedish meatballs, honey barbeque wings, stuffed mushrooms, and shrimp kabobs. And that's only the appetizer. Blaise told me to let you be surprised on the rest."

"Thanks so much, Bridget," I replied.

With all of this pomp and circumstance, it broke my heart that our baby wasn't expected to live after he or she was born. I fought back tears, threatening to fill my eyes once again. As I walked around the room looking for Blaise, I felt a hand on my shoulder. I turned around and was relieved to see Sheila. In the short period of time that she had moved in with us, I had really started to bond with her. She had a sweet and calming disposition that made me relax when she was around.

"How are you doing Faith?" Sheila asked.

"I'm hanging in there," I said. "But I'm looking for Blaise and I'm so thirsty."

"I knew you would be," Sheila said. She pulled out an ice-cold bottle of water and handed it to me with a straw. "The straw is so that you don't mess up your lipstick," she said.

"Sheila, thank you so much." I took a long sip of the

ice-cold water and exhaled. "This is exactly what I needed."

I studied Sheila's face and noticed anxiety. "Sheila are you alright?" I asked.

"It just hit me this morning that your parents are coming today, aren't they? I don't want it to be awkward when they see me."

"Sheila, don't worry about that. We're all adults." And at that moment I was able to see Kya's point of view. If my parents would be ok with being at the same event as Sheila, who actually had an affair with my dad, I could be alright with being at an event with Kya and Alfonso.

"Ok Faith," Sheila said. "Should I apologize to your mother or anything?"

"I don't think that's necessary," I said. "My mother has forgiven my father for all of that and it's under the blood."

Sheila looked puzzled as she walked away and I made a mental note to explain why the blood is so important to Christians.

Far in the distance, I could see Blaise talking to one of the musicians under the tent in the backyard. When I went outside and caught up with him he said, "Baby, you look beautiful. How are you feeling?"

"Thanks, honey. I'm feeling pretty good."

I looked Blaise up and down and admired how handsome he looked. He was dressed in a pair of khaki dress pants with a white short-sleeved dress shirt that accentuated all of the hard work he put in at the gym. My goodness, my man was fine.

Blaise put his hand on my stomach and leaned down to talk to the baby. "And how are you doing in there lil man?" I raised an eyebrow. Blaise grinned and said, "Oops, or lil mama? Either way, I'm just ready to find out what we're having."

I leaned over and whispered in Blaise's ear, "This is still so hard. We're doing all of this and what if--"

"We've got to trust in God, baby," Blaise replied. "We can either focus on our feelings, or we can focus on the facts. Today I'm focusing on the fact that you are pregnant with an active baby. Today I'm focusing on the fact that we have been married for one whole year." Blaise grabbed my hand and twirled me around. "And today I'm focusing on the fact that my wife is fine, and the doctor didn't give us any bedroom restrictions, amen?"

I giggled.

"There's that smile," Blaise said, leaning in to kiss me on the cheek. "Facts over feelings."

One of the vendors setting up an amplifier whisked Blaise away and I felt a tap on my shoulder.

I turned around and there was Kya looking like a million bucks.

I hugged her neck and did my best not to ruin my makeup for the umpteenth time that day.

"Faith you look so cute," Kya exclaimed. "Oh my

goodness, someday when I'm pregnant, I hope I can look this good."

"You're gonna make me blush," I joked.

Suddenly Kya's face looked somber and she leaned in to whisper in my ear, "I need to talk to you about something."

"Ok," I replied. "What is it? Are you alright?"

"I'm fine, but I wanted to know how you would feel about talking to Jude. He drove me here today--"

"Kya," I interjected.

"Just hear me out," Kya said. "Jude has a friend in the ministry who lives about fifteen minutes from here, so he's not planning on staying. But he *is* in the car and if you'll agree to it, he wanted to talk to you."

I sighed. I didn't want to talk to Alfonso ever again, but I felt like Kya was forcing me.

I looked around and spotted Blaise again. "Only if Blaise is with me," I said.

"Thank you so much, Faith. I'll be right back." Kya disappeared while I gave Blaise a heads up.

Blaise walked over to me. "What's up baby? Did I just see Kya walk by?"

"Yes. And she brought Alfonso."

"After you told her not to?"

"Well, technically she didn't. He just brought her here and is planning to go visit a friend of his who lives nearby."

Blaise nodded and I continued.

"But she said that he wants to talk to me if I'm ok with that."

"So what'd you tell her?" Blaise asked.

"I told her I'd talk to him only if you were with me."

"Why? So I can beat him up if he gets out of hand?" Blaise howled.

"Here they come," I said, pretending that I hadn't just been whispering about them.

"Hi guys," Kya said.

I looked beyond Kya and squinted. There was no way the guy behind her was Alfonso. Cornrows gone. Ripped physique gone. Even his light skin was gone. Kya told me that his medical condition had caused his skin color to darken a bit and now I could completely understand why she didn't recognize him. If it weren't for her telling me who he was, I would've walked right past him thinking he was a stranger. Then he spoke and I recognized his voice, but somehow that had changed too. He didn't sound as ignorant and thugged out like he did before. He spoke to Blaise first, while giving him the traditional black man handshake, slash hug.

"How's it going man?" Alfonso said. "My name is Jude."

"Nice to meet you, I'm Blaise."

Alfonso turned to look at me and I wanted to disappear into the ground. So many memories began swirling around in my head. The arguments, the frustrations, the physical parts of our relationship that never should've happened. If someone had told me that I'd be standing here today talking to him again in this setting, I would've told them that their pants were on fire.

"How are you, Faith? It's been a long time."

"It sure has, Alfonso."

"Actually I go by Jude now."

"That's right, Kya *did* mention that. Why are you going by your middle name again?"

"It's just my way of acknowledging the change that has taken place in my life. The scriptures are filled with people who were given different names after their conversion."

"Really? Like who?" I asked as Blaise nudged me.

But Alfonso answered. "Well, there's Jacob who became Israel, Abram who became Abraham, Sarai who became Sara, and Saul who became Paul. That's just to name a few off the top of my head. There may actually be more."

"Makes sense," Blaise said.

Alfonso continued. "So if you could please call me Jude, I'd appreciate it. I'm not the person that Alfonso represented and I don't ever plan to answer to that name again."

"Ok...Jude," I said.

"Thanks," Jude replied. "Faith I wanted to talk to you and I'm glad that you asked for your husband to be here because I wanted to apologize. I'm sorry for the ways that I hurt you when we dated. I'm sorry for the ways I defrauded you with an ungodly relationship, and I'm sorry for any disrespect that I showed you."

"Thanks, Jude," I said, stunned.

"And to Blaise. Brother, no disrespect. This is your wife now and I am in no way harboring any feelings based on the past."

"I appreciate that bro," Blaise said.

"And Faith I just want you to know that I understand you being skeptical of my relationship with Kya. I get it, trust me. But I can honestly say that God brought us together and I love Kya more than I love my own life. I mean that. You have my word that before God I will never display any of the same behavior with Kya that I displayed before I was a Christian."

Kya was dabbing tears from the corners of her eyes as I exchanged glances with Blaise.

"Wow, Jude," I said. "You definitely didn't have to say all of that, but I'm glad you did. Thank you."

"Alright, well I'm going to run," Jude said. "You all enjoy the party."

"You sure you don't want to stay?" Blaise asked.

"I told Pastor Cartwright that I was coming over so I want to honor my commitment, but I'll come by when I'm finished meeting with him."

Jude gave Kya a kiss on the forehead and left.

Kya turned to look at me and said, "See! Now, do you see what I was talking about Faith?"

"Girl," I said. "I'm speechless. I have never witnessed anything like that. He has truly changed, and he loves you in an incredible way. I can't believe I'm saying this, but I'm happy for you sis."

I hugged Kya and sighed.

"What's wrong?" Kya asked.

"It's a long story," I replied. "And if I start talking about it now, I'll start crying and I won't be able to stop."

"Oh ok," Kya said. "You and Blaise are good, right?"

"Girl yes. Blaise and I are solid."

"Ok good," Kya said. "Well whatever is going on, just remember Romans 8:28. God's got it, sis."

Kya disappeared into the house as I felt the strongest kick from the baby that I had ever felt. Tears stung my eyes as I held my hand to my stomach and felt another strong thump. It was devastating to think that in just a few short months our baby would be born only to die. I ran into the house as the tears began to flow all over again.

CHAPTER 18

There wasn't a cloud in sight as the warm breeze ushered in the laughter of friends and family, the mellow sounds of the band, and the aroma of shrimp kabobs, barbecued chicken, and mango salad, to name a few.

Faith was enjoying the coolness of the shade under the white tent that housed several white tables and chairs along with a stunning crystal chandelier that hung at the top.

Family and friends greeted my stunning bride and she flashed her best grin, but only I could see the pain behind her smile. The sadness in her eyes. Faith was a trooper and although she didn't want to host this celebration, she had agreed to it, to appease me. I didn't deserve her.

I made my way over to Faith and placed my hand around her growing waist. She turned to look at me and we communicated without words. With my eyes, I told her that I loved her and that it was going to be okay. Her eyes became misty and told me that she was relieved that I was by her side. I kissed her on the cheek as the photographer snapped a picture.

I whispered into Faith's ear, "It's going to be alright baby. Lord, please comfort my wife right now. Please fill her with your divine peace and grace. Thank you for the life that is growing within her right now and thank you in advance for what you're going to do through this situation. We trust you, Lord. In Jesus' name, Amen."

"Thank you, honey," Faith whispered.

"Let's just enjoy this moment," I said. "Right now we're here and it's a day to celebrate. Let's not let our fears of the future get in the way of the blessing of the present."

"You're right," Faith smiled. "Let's enjoy the right now."

With my hands still around Faith's waist, I pulled her close and felt a thump.

"Blaise, did you feel that?" Faith exclaimed. "The baby just kicked."

Faith and I laughed and the more we laughed, the more the baby kicked.

The afternoon was filled with rich laughter, live jazz, delectable eats, and warm conversation.

As we made our way to the cake table I grabbed the microphone and said, "Faith and I just want to thank all of you for coming out today to help us celebrate the birth of our first child, along with the first year of our marriage. We really appreciate it."

I looked up at Faith and she nodded. I knew what that nod meant.

"So everyone, there's something that we'd like to share about our little bundle of joy. With the exceptions of our immediate families, no one else here knows that at our ultrasound appointment a few days ago, they discovered..." my voice cracked as tears formed.

"Excuse me," I said. The crowd chimed in with various hums of "Take your time" and "It's alright".

"But as I was saying at our last ultrasound it was discovered that our little bundle has a mass on his or her brain, and there is no cerebellum in their brain. According to the doctor, medical science says that our baby will live for only about thirty minutes after being born."

There was a collective gasp heard around everyone in the tent as I continued.

"That's the report of the doctor." I paused and the entire room started clapping.

With tears in my eyes, I felt my faith in God more than I ever had before. I continued.

"Now I'm not saying that I know the outcome, but what I *am* saying is that I know the one who knows the outcome and his ways are perfect."

By now everyone was standing on their feet clapping, and passing around tissues to wipe the many teary eyes.

"So we are trusting God and having faith that He's going to do what's best. Come what may…" Faith rubbed my back as I hung my head and cried. "Come what may," I continued. "We are going to give God praise because He's worthy!"

Pops made his way up to the front of the tent and put his arm around me. I still felt some kind of way toward him for cheating on my mother, but he was still my rock and I needed his strength at that time.

I handed Pops the mic. He held it up to his mouth and said, "I feel led to say a prayer of thanksgiving over my son and daughter right now and for my little grandchild. Let's bow."

Pops prayed a water-walking, mountain-moving prayer that left everyone in that tent in tears and in a state of praise and thanksgiving. When he said, "Amen" I began singing,

"It is well," the crowd responded. "It is well."

"With my soul, with my soul."

The band joined in as we all sang, "It is well, it is well with my soul."

Our family and friends clapped, they cried and they praised. Faith cried both sets of her lashes off and everyone joined us in laughter as she flicked them into the garbage with her fingernail.

I grabbed the microphone and said, "Alright, who's

team boy? Let's hear it!" There was a round of applause and a chorus of cheers.

Faith grabbed the mic and said, "And who's team girl? Make some noise!" Just about every lady in the room howled, shouted, and clapped.

"Alright," Faith said. "Blaise, let's cut the cake and find out!"

I stood behind Faith, held the cake knife and cut into the white two-tiered butter cream frosting cake.

The entire crowd was reduced to a whisper as everyone waited with great anticipation to see what color the cake was.

As we sliced into the cake, blue candies spilled out and everyone erupted with applause and cheers as blue confetti and blue balloons fell from the roof of the tent.

I grabbed the microphone and shouted, "It's a boy!"

Tears blurred my vision as I looked out into the crowd and saw Faith's parents, her brothers, Sheila, Kya and Jude, my parents, my siblings, and extended family along with church members, bandmates and friends.

As the cheers began to die down, I walked back up to the front of the tent and watched Faith hugging her family and friends. Grabbing the microphone I said, "Can the lovely Mrs. Hawthorne please make her way to the front of the tent? Your man needs to have a word with you." There were howls, whistles, and applause as Faith made her way to the front.

As I began speaking, the band began playing "It's our Anniversary by Tony Toni Tone."

"As you all know," I said. "Today is also special because it's our anniversary. Our first anniversary to be exact. And one of the reasons that we're celebrating so much this year, is because most of you weren't at our wedding last year. And the reason you weren't at our wedding last year is that we had been dating and doing the long-distance thing so much that we were sick of it and just ready to be together. So I called my favorite party planner, Cierra Mitchell, wave at the people Cierra!"

Cierra was walking around giving orders from a headset when she stopped and waved.

I continued, "And Cierra helped us to pull together a small wedding for our immediate family only, so we knew that this year we'd have a celebration for our extended family and friends, so thank you, everyone, for coming. Now…" I turned to face Faith.

"To the lovely Mrs. Faith Hawthorne, the woman who makes me stick my chest out with pride, the woman who makes me feel like a king…"

The crowd was back on their feet howling and clapping as I went on.

"To the woman who's so fine, I can't stop thanking God that she's mine, to my queen, my lover, my baby mama! Happy Anniversary girl! I'd be nothing without you!"

The florist came up to the front of the tent and

presented Faith with two dozen tiffany blue calla lilies. In the center of the bouquet was a box from Tiffany's.

Faith's mouth dropped open.

"Blaise,"

"Go ahead and open your gift, baby."

Faith opened the box and gasped when she saw her gift. A platinum pendant necklace with the baby's ultrasound picture inside. I put the necklace around Faith's neck and Faith thanked me with a kiss.

I thought we were done with presentations, but Faith took the microphone and said, "My turn."

The audience roared once again as Faith spoke.

"To Blaise. You truly are my knight in shining armor, my priest, my provider, and my protector. Thank you for covering me in prayer, for being patient with me, and for constantly encouraging me. I thank God for this past year of marriage and I look forward to the next fifty years with you."

Faith reached under the top of the podium and pulled out a Rolex box.

I love collecting watches, but when I opened the box and saw the watch, it took everything in me to fight the tears threatening to fall.

The watch was silver, but the face of the watch was baby boy's ultrasound picture.

When I leaned over to kiss Faith she said, "Great minds think alike." We had basically gotten each other different variations of the same gift.

As we greeted our guests and enjoyed the fellowship of our loved ones, Pops pulled me aside.

"What's going on son?"

"What do you mean Pops?

"You've been distant with me ever since that day that you came over to talk to Mama and I about the drama in Faith's family."

I sighed. I really didn't want to tell Pops the truth, but he knew me too well for me to hide it, so I decided to lay it all out there. "Pops, when you told me that you and Mama had dealt with infidelity in your marriage I was kind of in shock. I mean, Mama is a gem. And I don't know who the mistress was, but I just couldn't wrap my mind around your decision to cheat."

Pops shook his head. "I didn't cheat on your mother, Blaise. Mama cheated on me."

I was so shocked that I actually had to take a seat.

"Blaise, finding out that your mother had an extra-marital affair was the hardest thing I've ever gone through in this life. It took me a long time to extend grace and to forgive her, but through that experience, the Holy Spirit showed me that as the husband I had dropped the ball."

"How so Pops? Nothing you did gave Mama the excuse to go out and cheat."

"No it didn't, but I'm the spiritual leader of my home and I wasn't leading my family spiritually at all. Your mother used to ask me to pray with her, and I would always find an excuse as to why I couldn't. She used to ask me to take her to marriage conferences and many other marital events through our church, but I always found a way to stay home. What I didn't realize is that I was slowly pushing your mother away. Not saying that she was off the hook for what she did, but I definitely played a part as the leader of our home."

I was silent for a moment and then said, "Pops how did you manage to truly let that go and not hold Mama's sin over her head? Didn't you feel like you were better than her, because you didn't fall into sexual temptation?"

"Son, Isaiah 64:6 says that 'All our righteousness are as filthy rags…' That basically means that compared to the holiness of God, even our very best is filthy to him. There is nothing good about us apart from Christ, so none of us are authorized to boast or to feel like we're better than anyone else. Does that make sense?"

"It sure does Pops," I replied.

"And do me a favor," Pops said. "Please don't look at your mother any differently because of what I told you. She's a jewel who I really don't even deserve and that affair happened thirty years ago."

"I'll never look at Mama any different," I said.

"That's my boy," Pops said, leaning in to kiss me on the cheek.

That night after the cleaning crew put the yard back together and all of the guests had gone home, I waited impatiently for Faith to say goodnight to Sheila in her guest suite downstairs.

When Faith walked into the bedroom, she plopped down onto the bed and exhaled.

"What a day," she said.

"So you liked the party after all, huh?"

"It was perfect," Faith said.

Her grin lit up the room as she stood up and walked to the bathroom.

I ran the water in the shower as Faith stood in front of the mirror, removing the baby's breath and confetti from her hair.

I undressed, got into the shower and said to Faith, "care to join me?"

Faith flashed a sly grin, undressed and joined me in the shower.

I held my wife under the warm rain and massaged co-wash into her hair. I massaged her scalp and her temples and poured body wash onto a loofa that I used to massage her back and her shoulders. With her back against my chest, I leaned over and rubbed her stomach. Baby boy said hello with a kick and I thought my heart was going to explode.

"I love him so much already," I whispered.

"I know," Faith whispered back.

After I finished rinsing Faith's hair and back, she returned the favor massaging body wash into my shoulders and back.

When we finished showering we become one in our bed and held each other for the rest of the night.

It was one of the happiest days of my life.

CHAPTER 19

*A*fter the amazing time of worship and prayer that we had at the gender reveal, you'd think that I wouldn't be a ball of nerves less than twenty-four hours later, but alas, here I was, literally trembling with fear. I worried if the baby didn't move enough. I worried if the baby moved too much. I worried that I wasn't eating enough vegetables, I worried that the baby would develop any number of health issues in addition to the ones he already had. The worry and anxiety were consuming me to the point of torture.

I looked at the time on the clock sitting on the nightstand. *5:06 am*

What would Granny C do if she couldn't sleep in the wee hours of the morning?

I pulled my journal out of the nightstand stand and began writing.

Where are you God when the moon is awake and the

sun is down low and my heart starts to break? Where are you God when life's trials steal my peace, and the rain barrels down and the storms will not cease? Where are you God when my burdens are strong, and the day is too short, but the nights are so long? Oh Lord, you are there. Where you always were. I know that you care. Strengthen my faith in the stillness of the night. Restore my joy in the power of your might. All I need is mustard seed Faith, for your light to shine down on the path that I take. Thank you, Lord for covering me, for being my help in the stormy seas.

I put my journal away and noticed Blaise watching me.

"You okay baby?"

"I'm a bit better now," I replied. "I just keep worrying about the baby."

"I know. Me too."

"Really Blaise? But you seemed so confident."

"I am confident, but I'm still human. It reminds me of a scripture passage in Mark chapter nine. There was a boy who had an evil spirit that caused him to lose his speech and foam at the mouth. The boy's father brought him to the disciples and asked them to heal the boy, but no matter what the disciples did, they couldn't heal him. Finally, Jesus stepped in and told the father he needed to believe, to which the father replied, 'I believe, but help my unbelief.' That's how I feel right now, Faith. I believe that God's ways are beyond our ways and that ultimately his plan for us is perfect, but I still struggle with unbelief and fear as I imagine what the future may hold."

"So what's the solution?" I asked.

"Well in that same scripture passage, after Jesus healed the young boy, the disciples asked Jesus why they weren't able to heal him. Jesus replied that there are certain spirits that can only be driven away through prayer and fasting. Faith I think that until the baby is born, we need to exercise our faith through prayer and fasting on a regular basis. It's the only way that we'll be strong enough to overcome the looming anxiety that this trial is bringing into our lives."

"Alright," I said. "I'll fast from social media and from television since I can't fast from food right now."

"Ok," Blaise said. "Then I'm going to fast from social media, television, and I'm going to fast from food every Wednesday from now until the baby is born."

"Sounds good," I said.

There was silence for a moment and then Blaise said, "Let's pray right now."

We held hands as Blaise prayed, "Father we believe you, but please help the parts of us that still don't believe. Help us to trust your will, and to rely on the facts versus our feelings. God, we don't know what your will is, but we're praying for a miracle. Please heal our baby boy Father. I'm praying that during the next ultrasound the mass on his brain will be gone and that he will be completely healthy. Use us to share the testimony of your healing power with others. Finally, Lord, help us to praise you and give you glory no matter what the outcome is because you are worthy of all the praise we can muster. Thank you in Jesus name we pray, Amen."

When I got back into bed, nothing had changed but a peace swept over me that put me fast asleep.

CHAPTER 20

"Stand up and let me see you!" Kya squealed over facetime.

I stood up and turned around so Kya could get the full view of my belly.

"And how many weeks are you now?"

"Thirty-five weeks," I replied.

"Almost to the finish line," Kya said. "Are you nervous?"

"It comes in waves. Our prayer had been that the mass on the baby's brain would be gone by now, but as of our last ultrasound at thirty-four weeks, it was still there."

"I'm sorry sis," Kya said. "Jude and I are still praying for a miracle."

"Thanks. We need all the prayers that we can get."

"How are things going with Sheila?" Kya asked.

"Girl, I didn't tell you?"

"No," Kya exclaimed. "What happened?"

I told Kya about one of the most dynamic Sunday services I had ever been a part of.

Pastor Albright was preaching from Hebrews 9:22b which says "Without the shedding of blood there will be no remission of sins." "You see brothers and sisters," Pastor Albright said. "The Old Testament saints had to offer up a sacrifice to cover their sins. They would have to sacrifice an animal that had no blemishes on it, and that served as their sacrifice. So fast forward years later and Jesus came to earth to pay the ultimate sacrifice for all of us. Turn in your Bibles to John chapter one and verse twenty-nine. When John saw Jesus he said, 'Behold the Lamb of God who takes away the sins of the world'. So John recognized Jesus as the ultimate Lamb! The perfect Lamb who would shed his blood on Calvary's cross so that all of us could be made whole. After Jesus took on all of our sins on the cross and shed his blood for us, no one else had to offer up a sacrifice of an animal to cover their sins. We see in Romans 6:23 that the wages of sin is death, but the gift of God is eternal life through Jesus Christ our Lord. So again that verse is just explaining that a penalty needed to be paid to cover our sins, and being that none of us is perfect, Jesus was the only one who could've laid down his life for the sins of mankind. And now because of his sacrifice, all we have to do to obtain eternal life, is to believe in what he did on the cross. But you know what the best news is saints? The best news is that after he died on the cross, he didn't stay there. Three days later, he got up and rose again like new, with all power in his hands! And because he lives, I can face tomorrow! Because he lives, all fear is gone! Because I know he holds the future! And life is worth the living just because he lives!"

By the time Pastor Albright finished preaching, I looked at Sheila and she had tears streaming down her face. She went forward to the altar call and said, "I've been living my life for me. That's the only way I've ever lived and it's made me miserable. Today I want to start living my life for God! I believe that he died on the cross for my sins and I believe that he rose again. I know that he did that for me so that if I believe in him I *will* be saved, and one day when I take my last breath, I *will* be in heaven with him. Death doesn't seem as scary anymore, because I know where I'm going."

Blaise and I were in tears as the congregation erupted in praise and worship over the salvation of my biological mother.

"My God," Kya exclaimed. "That's beautiful."

"And the first thing Sheila did after church was apologize to Blaise and I."

"What did she apologize for?"

"She apologized for a couple of reasons. So when she first came to stay with us she had a black eye and her face was swollen. She told us it was because she fell down the steps, but the truth of the matter was that her ex-boyfriend had beat her up really bad."

"Aww naw,"

"Right."

"And the other reason she apologized is because apparently her plan was to mooch off of us when she first came here to live. She never did though. Once she started getting to know us she didn't have the heart to."

"It sounds like she's really a genuine person."

"She is," I said. "Moving her in with us is one of the best things we've ever done."

"So how is work?" Kya asked. "Will you be going on maternity leave soon?"

"Girl I quit that job a month ago."

"Why?"

"I realized that I was no longer fulfilled in it, and with all of the health issues with the baby, I wanted to be able to focus on maintaining a healthy pregnancy."

"Well good for you Faith," Kya said. "It's about time you quit your job and learn to relax. It's not like you need the money."

Suddenly I felt a gush of fluid that made me gasp.

"Faith, what's wrong?" Kya asked.

"I think my water just broke! And it's too early!" I cried.

"Oh no," Kya said. "Ok keep calm. Is Blaise home?"

"Yes, I need to go get Blaise."

"Ok, praying for you sis. Please keep me posted."

As I hung up with Kya, Blaise walked into the bedroom. When he saw my face he knew that something was wrong.

"Faith, what's wrong?" Blaise rushed to the bed where I was sitting.

"I think my water just broke."

"Let's get to the hospital," Blaise said.

I stood up to try to get my shoes on, but more water gushed out, and I had the first contraction that brought me to my knees.

Blaise grabbed my shoes, threw them in a bag, picked me up and carried me to the car.

"Wait. What about Sheila?" I asked.

"Sheila's gone shopping with some of the ladies from church, remember?"

"That's right," I panted.

As Blaise weaved in and out of traffic, he said, "Have you felt the baby move at all?"

"Not once in the last hour," I said, with tears welling up in my eyes.

"Well, you know what?" Blaise said. "No matter what the outcome is today, we are going to rejoice in knowing that Love was delivered to us on this day. Whether he's awake or sleeping. This baby has brought us so much love, and for that, we will be thankful no matter what."

As we pulled into the hospital parking lot, Blaise swiped at the tears streaming down his face.

Inside the hospital, I was quickly taken to Labor & Delivery where I was attached to several monitors and dopplers in hopes of finding the baby's heartbeat.

After what felt like an eternity, the baby's heartbeat was detected on the monitor.

"Praise God," Blaise sighed. "Baby, you okay?"

In the most excruciating pain that I had ever experienced in my life, all I could do was shake my head no.

"Let's do the breathing they showed us in the birthing class," Blaise said.

So I held Blaise's hand and did the breathing exercises, which did absolutely nothing for the pain. A minute later, a tall slender woman with porcelain skin, green eyes, and hair the color of fire walked in. She said, "Faith are you ready for an epidural hun?"

I had always said that I would get an epidural when I went into labor, and that's exactly how I responded to the nurse. "Yes please," was my faint reply.

"Let's see how far dilated you are," the nurse said. She checked me and said, "Whoa! It's time to have a baby."

"Wait," Blaise said. "It's time to push?"

"It sure is," Dr. Woods replied as she walked into the room, putting her latex gloves on.

One nurse held my left foot, while Blaise held my right foot. Dr. Woods looked at me and said, "Ok Faith, on the count of three, I want you to bear down and push as hard as you can for ten seconds, and then you're going to take a little break and then do it again, ok?"

I nodded my head in agreement.

"Ok Faith. One, two, three."

I pushed with all my might for ten seconds, then took a break just like Dr. Woods said, and repeated. I lost track of how many times we repeated that cycle, but after what felt like forever, I could feel the baby crowning.

"You're doing great, baby," Blaise said. "Push one more time."

I pushed with all my might and wailed when I felt the baby pass completely through the birthing canal.

"Congratulations, Faith. He's here," said Dr. Woods.

I held my breath because I didn't hear a cry. I looked at Blaise. "Why is he not crying?" I asked in a panic.

"Is he alright doc?" Blaise asked.

Dr. Woods didn't speak a word, they just whisked our son over to the bright lights and started working on him. I hadn't even had a chance to get a good look at him yet.

With each second that passed without hearing a cry, my heart pounded harder. Blaise began praying out loud with his arms wrapped around me as I trembled like a leaf.

"Heal our son, God. Please, Lord. In Jesus Name, please heal our baby."

And then we heard it. The most beautiful sound I had ever witnessed.

Tears streamed down our faces as Dr. Woods brought the baby to me and laid him on my chest. The second his face landed on my chest he began rooting in search of my breast. He latched on strong and whimpered as he suckled.

"Did anyone tell you his measurements?" a nurse asked.

"No," Blaise said. "And it was so scary in the beginning, we didn't think to ask."

"He's five lbs twelve ounces and is twenty inches long," the nurse replied.

As relieved as we were that the baby had survived the birthing process, our hearts were struck with fear remembering the original prognosis. With the mass on his brain and without a cerebellum, he would live no longer than thirty minutes.

"Dr. Woods," Blaise said. "So do we know what his condition is? I mean will you all test him or what? What do we do now?"

Dr. Woods said, "Just love on him and enjoy him. We're going to go and let you all have some privacy."

Blaise's parents were in the waiting room along with Sheila and while we knew they were anxious to see our son, we wanted to spend as much time with him as possible. We just didn't know when he would take his last breath. We sang to him, we prayed over him, we held him and we kissed him.

It felt like only a couple minutes had passed, but Blaise looked at the clock and said, "It's been thirty-five minutes since he's been born and he's still going strong."

We studied his features and could see a mixture of

both of us. He had Blaise's chin and my cheeks. He had Blaise's long hands and feet and my and Sheila's eyes.

He had a head full of jet black hair and judging from his fingertips and around his ears, he'd end up being Blaise's chestnut complexion.

Dr. Woods walked back in the room an hour later and said, "We'd like to take your little guy for an ultrasound to see how he's doing. Is that alright Mommy and Daddy?"

Blaise took the baby with the Doctor while I stayed behind resting. I drifted off to sleep and when I woke up Blaise was sitting next to me, holding the baby and sobbing.

My heart sank.

"Blaise, oh my goodness, what did they say?"

Blaise took a moment to compose himself. "They said that it's a miracle, Faith. The mass on his brain is gone and his brain is perfectly fine. It's a miracle."

In tears, I began to sing and Blaise joined me, "Praise God from whom all blessings flow, praise him all creatures here below. Praise him above ye heavenly hosts. Praise Father Son and Holy Ghost. Amen."

That evening I woke up from a nap to the sound of Blaise singing *Jesus Loves Me* to the cutest little baby on earth. But I guess I'm biased. Blaise turned around and saw that I was awake and said, "Look, baby. Mommy's awake." He eased down next to me in the bed and said, "We sure did make a pretty baby."

I flashed a weak smile. "I just can't wait until I feel like myself again."

"You'll get there baby. You just let me know what you need, and I got you."

Blaise kissed me on the cheek, and said, "Faith I fell deeper in love with you today. Seeing you bring our son into the world was the most beautiful thing I've ever seen."

"Thanks honey."

There was a knock at the door and Blaise's parents walked in along with all three of my parents.

"Congratulations!" they beamed in unison as they passed the baby around.

Sheila raised her hand and said, "Excuse me, everyone. I just wanted to take the time to thank each of you for welcoming me into the family, but especially you, Lorraine. You stepped in and raised Faith over the years, when you didn't have to and I thank God for you."

Mom and Dad both leaned over and hugged Sheila and I felt like I needed to pinch myself. This time last year I was filled with bitterness toward Sheila for abandoning me, and I was trying to establish a bond with my parents after being so angry with them over keeping the secret of my real mom away from me. Now here I sat with my dad, my mom who raised me and a bonus mom who delivered me. The power of God never ceased to amaze me.

Pops Hawthorne snapped me out of my daydream

by saying, "So what did y'all name the baby? I need to know the name of my new grandson."

Blaise spoke up with pride. "We named him Davin Michael Hawthorne. Michael means 'who is like God' and Davin means 'love'. So today is extra special," Blaise said, holding Davin up. "Here is the family's new gift. Love, Delivered."

DISCUSSION QUESTIONS

1. Faith is faced with the complexities of her estranged mother coming back into her life. Have you ever been faced with a similar issue? How did you handle it? Did Faith handle it well?

2. Faith and Kya struggle to see eye to eye over Kya wanting to date Faith's ex. Is that always a no-no or should exceptions be made sometimes? Have you been in that situation before? And if so, how did you handle it?

3. Pastor Albright preached a sermon about forgiveness that convicted Faith. Have you ever struggled with forgiveness? If so how did you handle it?

4. Blaise struggles with the revelation that his parent's marriage hasn't always been perfect.

Was he foolish to let the past bother him? Why or why not?

5. When Faith and Blaise received tragic news about their baby, Blaise tried his best to remain positive. Was he being insensitive to Faith in doing that? How do you handle tragedy?

6. Blaise spared no expense for the gender reveal/anniversary celebration. What was your favorite part of the celebration?

7. Pops Hawthorne talks to Blaise a bit more in-depth about the infidelity in his marriage. Do you think it's possible for a marriage to completely thrive after adultery?

8. After a great time of prayer that Faith and Blaise had at the gender reveal party, Faith woke up the next morning just as worried as ever. Has anything like that ever happened to you? What causes a Christian to give their worries to God only to begin worrying again and is there any way to stop it?

9. Several times throughout the book Blaise prays with his wife. How important do you think it is to have a Godly husband? In what ways do you think their marriage would've been different if Blaise wasn't close to God?

10. At the end of the book, Faith and Blaise sing a song of praise unto God. How important

do you think it is to give God praise for
answered prayer? Why or why not?

Made in the USA
Monee, IL
27 January 2020